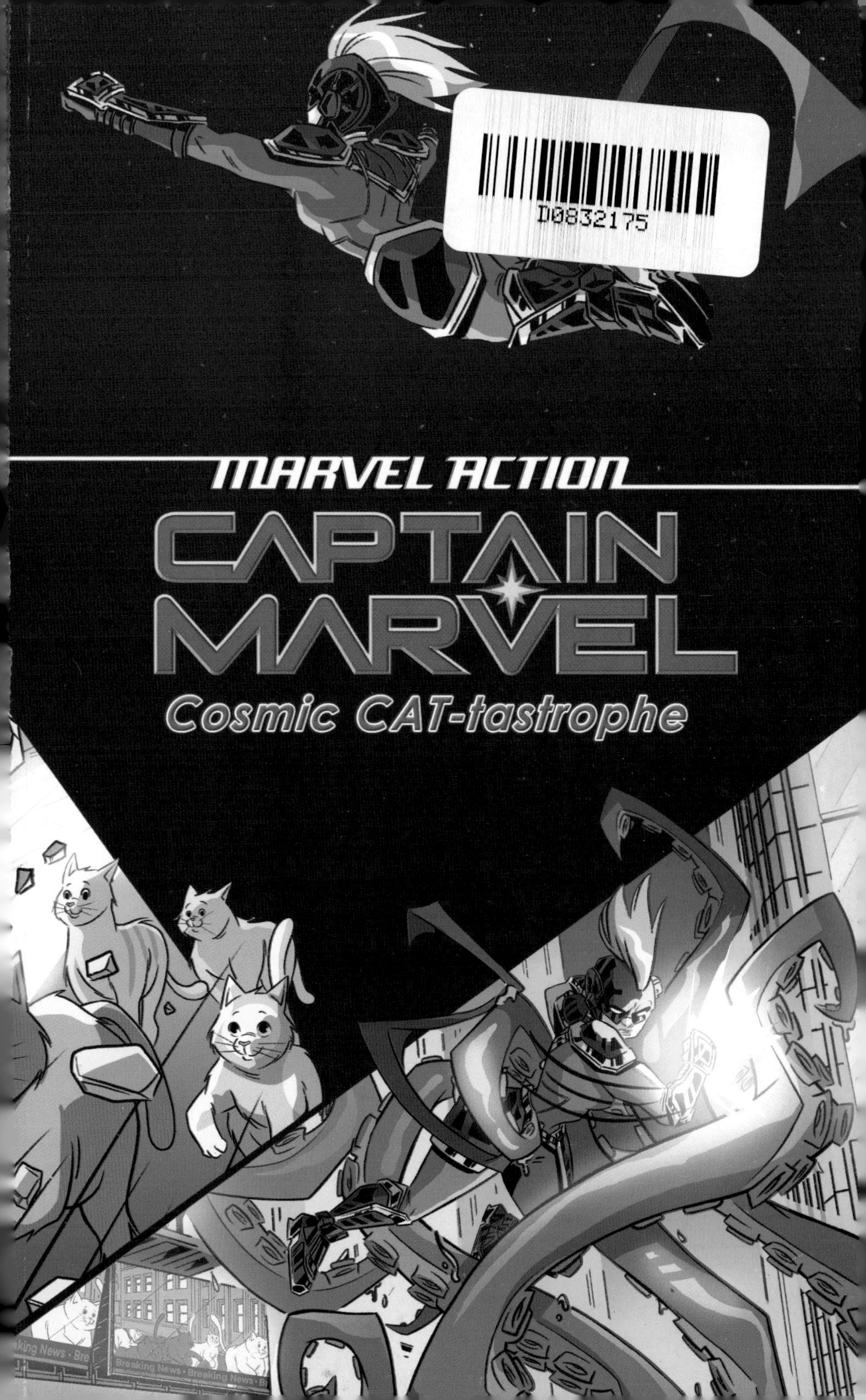
MARVEL ACTION
CAPTAIN MARVEL
Cosmic CAT-tastrophe
Breaking News • Breaking News

MARVEL — MARVEL ACTION

CAPTAIN MARVEL

Marvel Publishing:

Jeff Youngquist: VP Production & Special Projects
Caitlin O'Connell: Assistant Editor, Special Projects
Sven Larsen: Director, Licensed Publishing
David Gabriel: SVP Print, Sales & Marketing
C.B. Cebulski: Editor In Chief
Joe Quesada: Chief Creative Officer
Dan Buckley: President, Marvel Entertainment
Alan Fine: Executive Producer

IDW Publishing:

IDW

Cover Art by
SWEENEY BOO

Series Edits by
MEGAN BROWN
and **BOBBY CURNOW**

Collection Edits
JUSTIN EISINGER
and **ALONZO SIMON**

Collection Design
CHRISTA MIESNER

Chris Ryall, President and Publisher/CCO
Cara Morrison, Chief Financial Officer
Matt Ruzicka, Chief Accounting Officer
David Hedgecock, Associate Publisher
John Barber, Editor-In-Chief
Justin Eisinger, Editorial Director, Graphic Novels & Collections
Jerry Bennington, VP of New Product Development
Lorelei Bunjes, VP of Digital Services
Jud Meyers, Sales Director
Anna Morrow, Marketing Director
Tara McCrillis, Director of Design & Production
Mike Ford, Director of Operations
Rebekah Cahalin, General Manager
Ted Adams and Robbie Robbins, Founders of IDW

ISBN: 978-1-68405-624-8   23 22 21 20   1 2 3 4

Special thanks: **Sana Amanat and Sarah Brunstad**

MARVEL ACTION: CAPTAIN MARVEL: COSMIC CAT-TASTROPHE (BOOK 1). MARCH 2020. FIRST PRINTING. © 2020 MARVEL. The IDW logo is registered in the U.S. Patent and Trademark Office. IDW Publishing, a division of Idea and Design Works, LLC. Editorial offices: 2765 Truxtun Road, San Diego, CA 92106. Any similarities to persons living or dead are purely coincidental. With the exception of artwork used for review purposes, none of the contents of this publication may be reprinted without the permission of Idea and Design Works, LLC.

Printed in Korea.

IDW Publishing does not read or accept unsolicited submissions of ideas, stories, or artwork.

Originally published as MARVEL ACTION: CAPTAIN MARVEL issues #1–3.

For international rights, contact licensing@idwpublishing.com

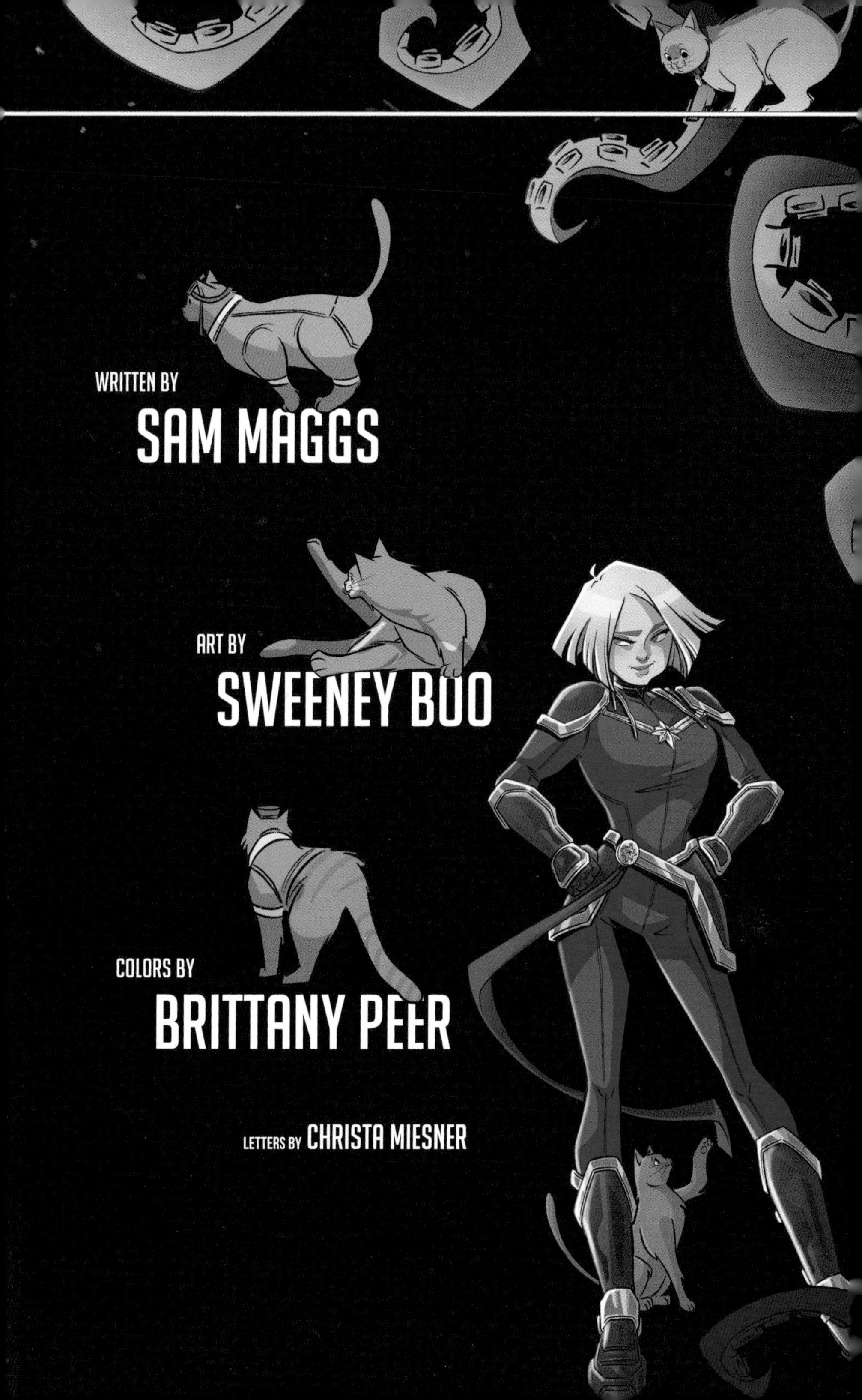
WRITTEN BY
SAM MAGGS
ART BY
SWEENEY BOO
COLORS BY
BRITTANY PEER
LETTERS BY CHRISTA MIESNER

ART BY: SWEENEY BOO

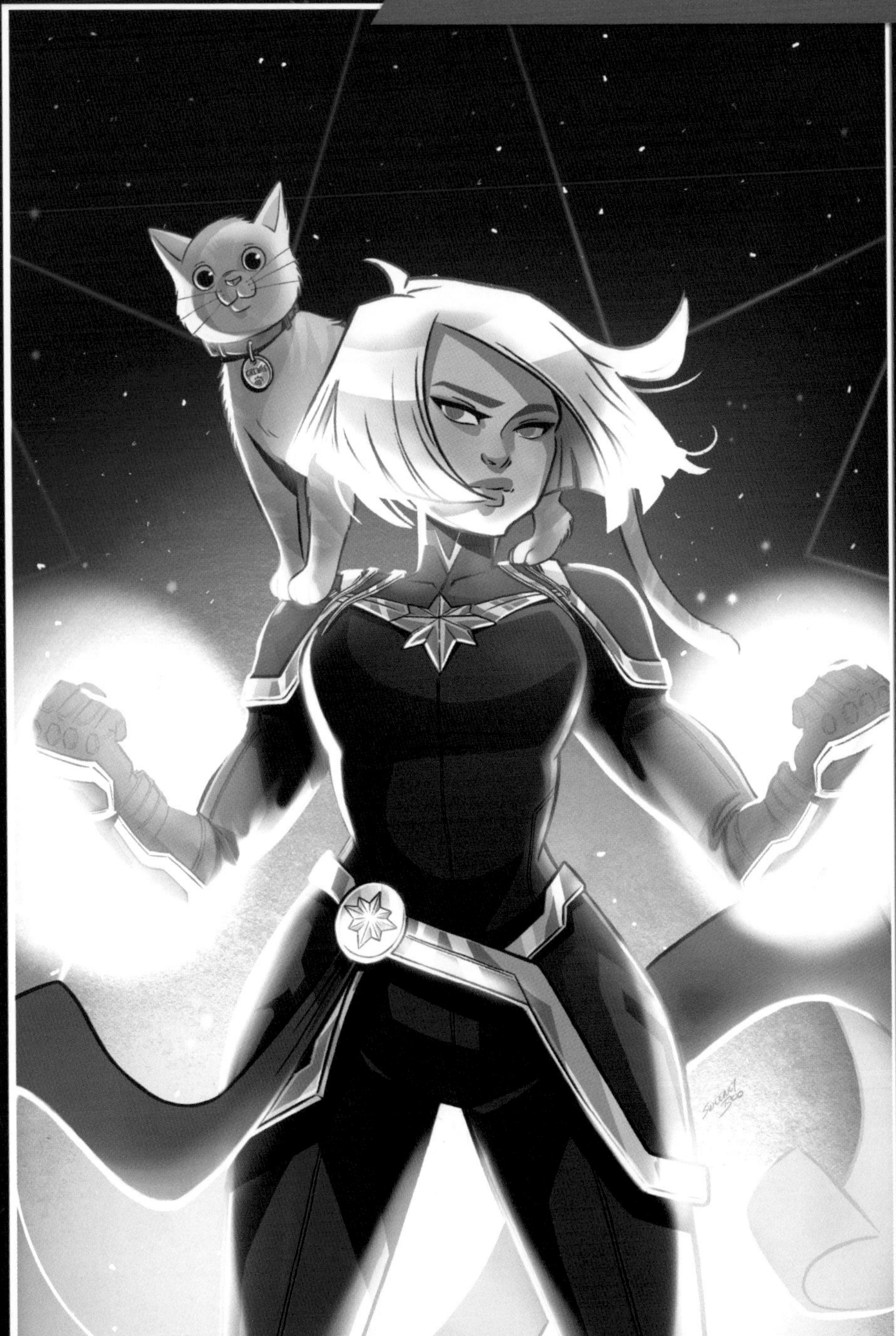

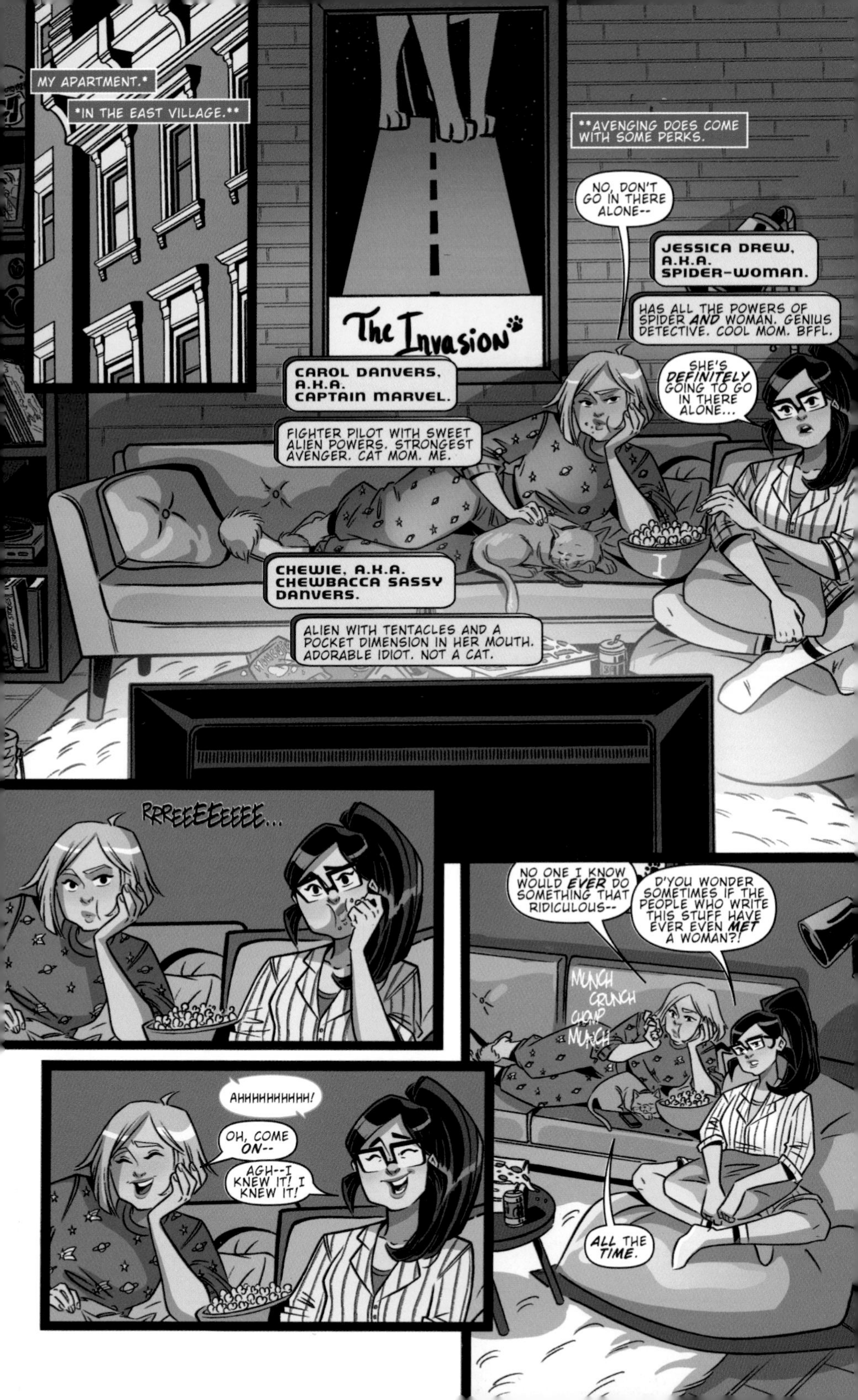

MY APARTMENT.*
*IN THE EAST VILLAGE.**
**AVENGING DOES COME WITH SOME PERKS.
NO, DON'T GO IN THERE ALONE--
JESSICA DREW, A.K.A. SPIDER-WOMAN.
HAS ALL THE POWERS OF SPIDER AND WOMAN. GENIUS DETECTIVE. COOL MOM. BFFL.
The Invasion
CAROL DANVERS, A.K.A. CAPTAIN MARVEL.
SHE'S DEFINITELY GOING TO GO IN THERE ALONE...
FIGHTER PILOT WITH SWEET ALIEN POWERS. STRONGEST AVENGER. CAT MOM. ME.
CHEWIE, A.K.A. CHEWBACCA SASSY DANVERS.
ALIEN WITH TENTACLES AND A POCKET DIMENSION IN HER MOUTH. ADORABLE IDIOT. NOT A CAT.
RRREEEEEEEEE...
NO ONE I KNOW WOULD EVER DO SOMETHING THAT RIDICULOUS--
D'YOU WONDER SOMETIMES IF THE PEOPLE WHO WRITE THIS STUFF HAVE EVER EVEN MET A WOMAN?!
MUNCH CRUNCH CHOMP MUNCH
ALL THE TIME.
AHHHHHHHHHH!
OH, COME ON--
AGH--I KNEW IT! I KNEW IT!

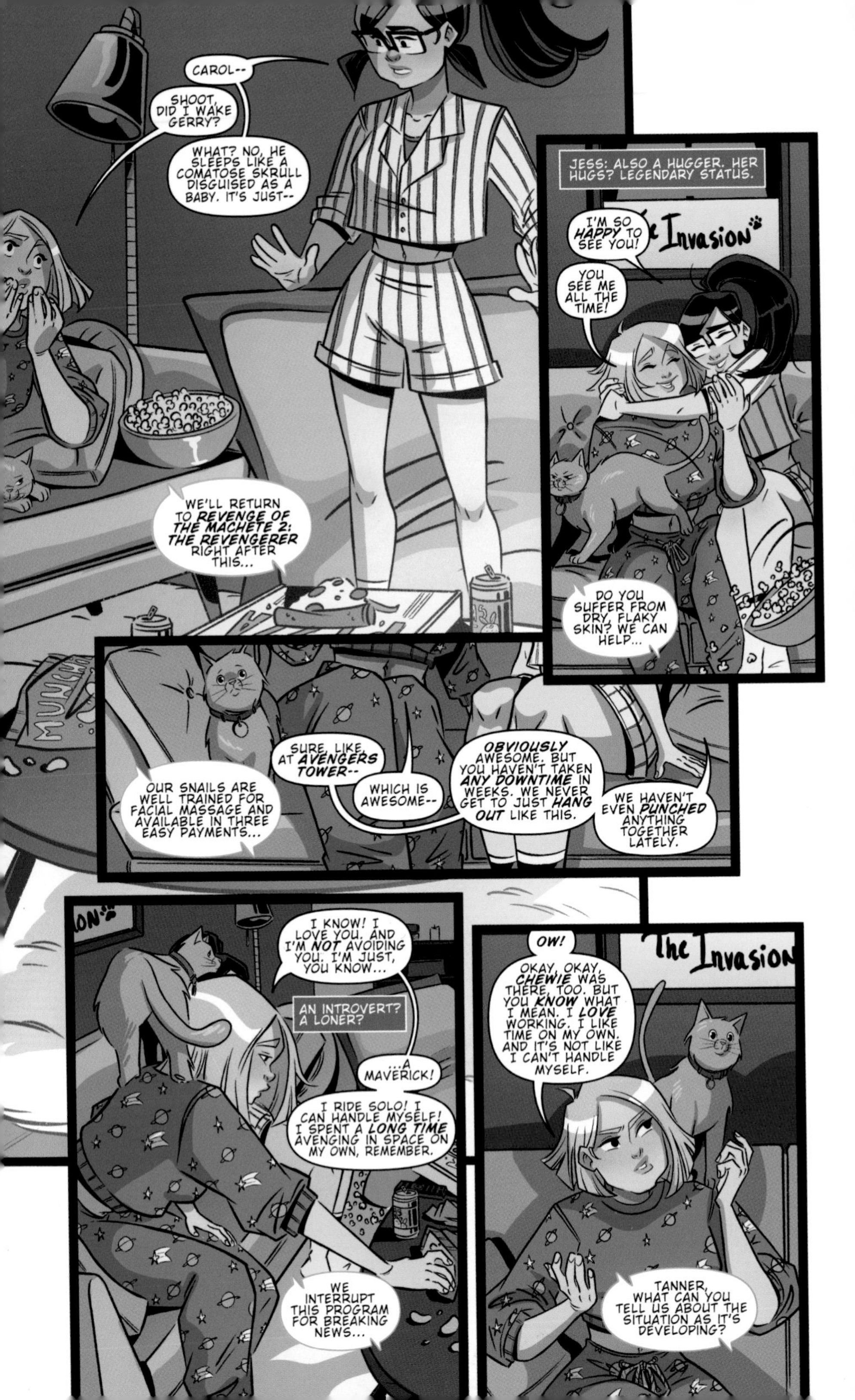
CAROL--
SHOOT, DID I WAKE GERRY?
WHAT? NO, HE SLEEPS LIKE A COMATOSE SKRULL DISGUISED AS A BABY. IT'S JUST--
WE'LL RETURN TO REVENGE OF THE MACHETE 2: THE REVENGERER RIGHT AFTER THIS...
JESS: ALSO A HUGGER. HER HUGS? LEGENDARY STATUS.
I'M SO HAPPY TO SEE YOU!
YOU SEE ME ALL THE TIME!
The Invasion
DO YOU SUFFER FROM DRY, FLAKY SKIN? WE CAN HELP...
MUNCH
OUR SNAILS ARE WELL TRAINED FOR FACIAL MASSAGE AND AVAILABLE IN THREE EASY PAYMENTS...
SURE, LIKE, AT AVENGERS TOWER--
WHICH IS AWESOME--
OBVIOUSLY AWESOME. BUT YOU HAVEN'T TAKEN ANY DOWNTIME IN WEEKS. WE NEVER GET TO JUST HANG OUT LIKE THIS.
WE HAVEN'T EVEN PUNCHED ANYTHING TOGETHER LATELY.
I KNOW! I LOVE YOU. AND I'M NOT AVOIDING YOU. I'M JUST, YOU KNOW...
AN INTROVERT? A LONER?
...A MAVERICK!
I RIDE SOLO! I CAN HANDLE MYSELF! I SPENT A LONG TIME AVENGING IN SPACE ON MY OWN, REMEMBER.
WE INTERRUPT THIS PROGRAM FOR BREAKING NEWS...
OW!
OKAY, OKAY, CHEWIE WAS THERE, TOO. BUT YOU KNOW WHAT I MEAN. I LOVE WORKING. I LIKE TIME ON MY OWN. AND IT'S NOT LIKE I CAN'T HANDLE MYSELF.
The Invasion
TANNER, WHAT CAN YOU TELL US ABOUT THE SITUATION AS IT'S DEVELOPING?

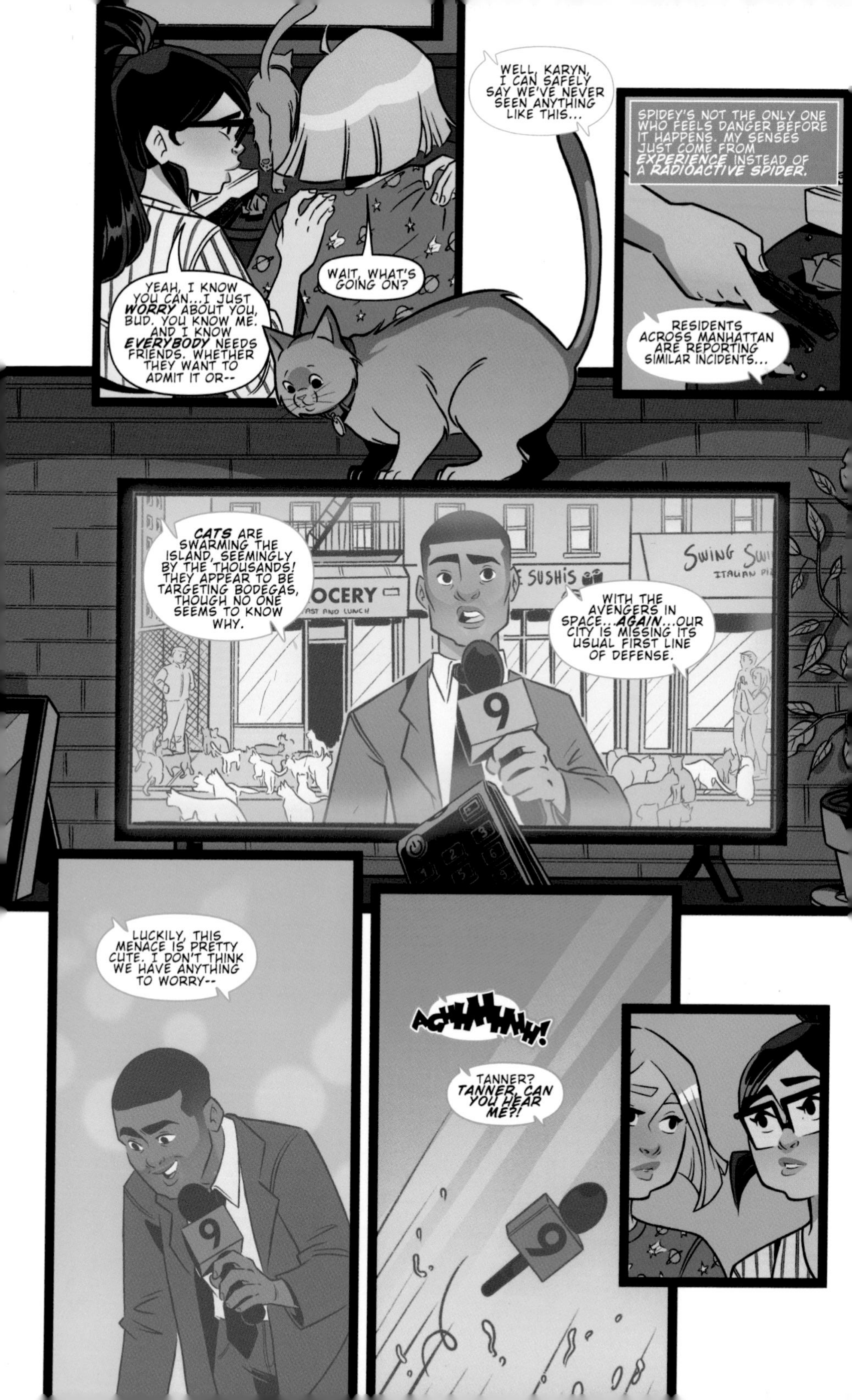
WELL, KARYN, I CAN SAFELY SAY WE'VE NEVER SEEN ANYTHING LIKE THIS...
YEAH, I KNOW YOU CAN...I JUST WORRY ABOUT YOU, BUD. YOU KNOW ME. AND I KNOW EVERYBODY NEEDS FRIENDS. WHETHER THEY WANT TO ADMIT IT OR--
WAIT, WHAT'S GOING ON?
SPIDEY'S NOT THE ONLY ONE WHO FEELS DANGER BEFORE IT HAPPENS. MY SENSES JUST COME FROM EXPERIENCE INSTEAD OF A RADIOACTIVE SPIDER.
RESIDENTS ACROSS MANHATTAN ARE REPORTING SIMILAR INCIDENTS...
CATS ARE SWARMING THE ISLAND, SEEMINGLY BY THE THOUSANDS! THEY APPEAR TO BE TARGETING BODEGAS, THOUGH NO ONE SEEMS TO KNOW WHY.
WITH THE AVENGERS IN SPACE...AGAIN...OUR CITY IS MISSING ITS USUAL FIRST LINE OF DEFENSE.
LUCKILY, THIS MENACE IS PRETTY CUTE. I DON'T THINK WE HAVE ANYTHING TO WORRY--
ACHHHHHHH!
TANNER? TANNER, CAN YOU HEAR ME?!

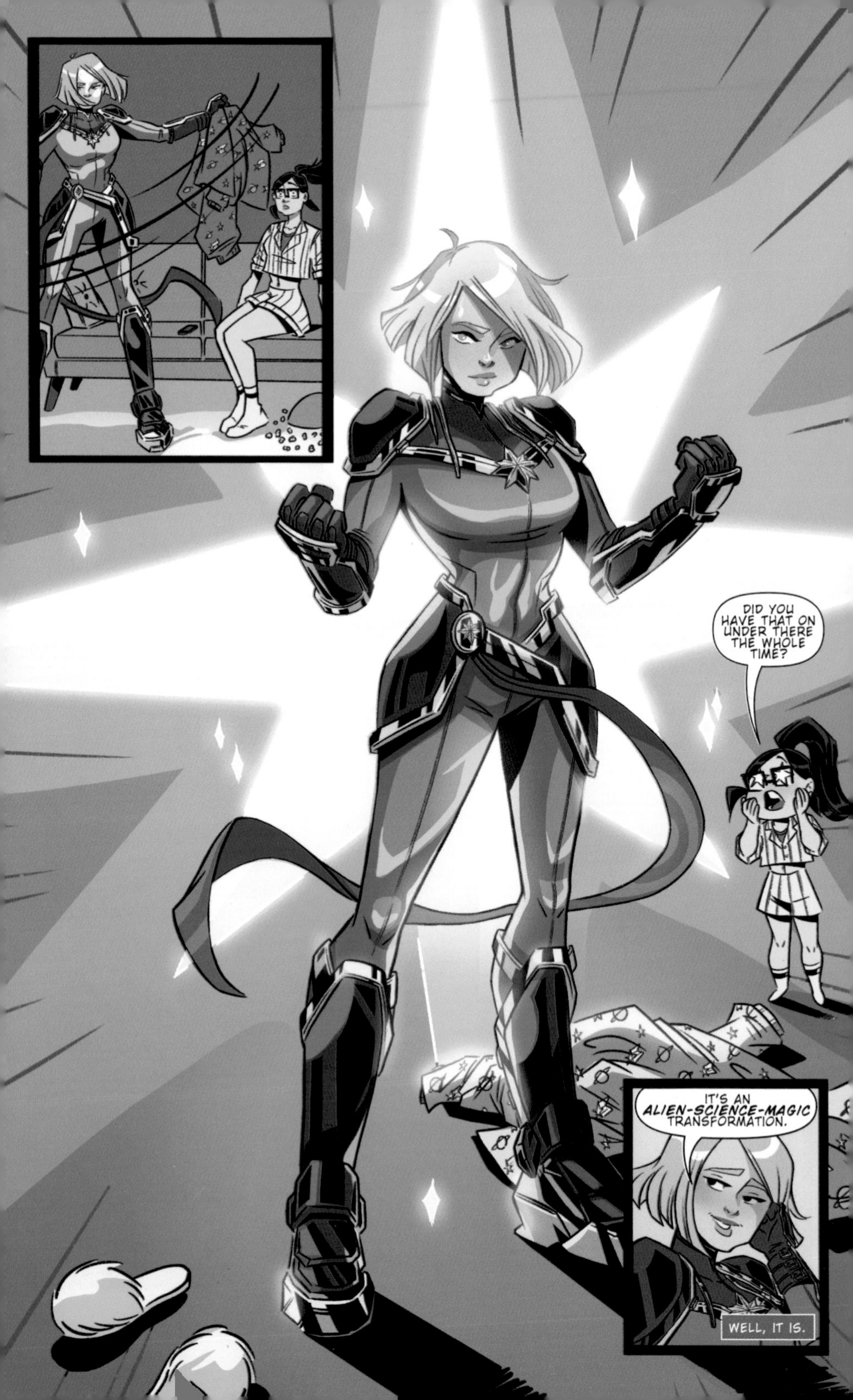
DID YOU HAVE THAT ON UNDER THERE THE WHOLE TIME?
IT'S AN ALIEN-SCIENCE-MAGIC TRANSFORMATION.
WELL, IT IS.

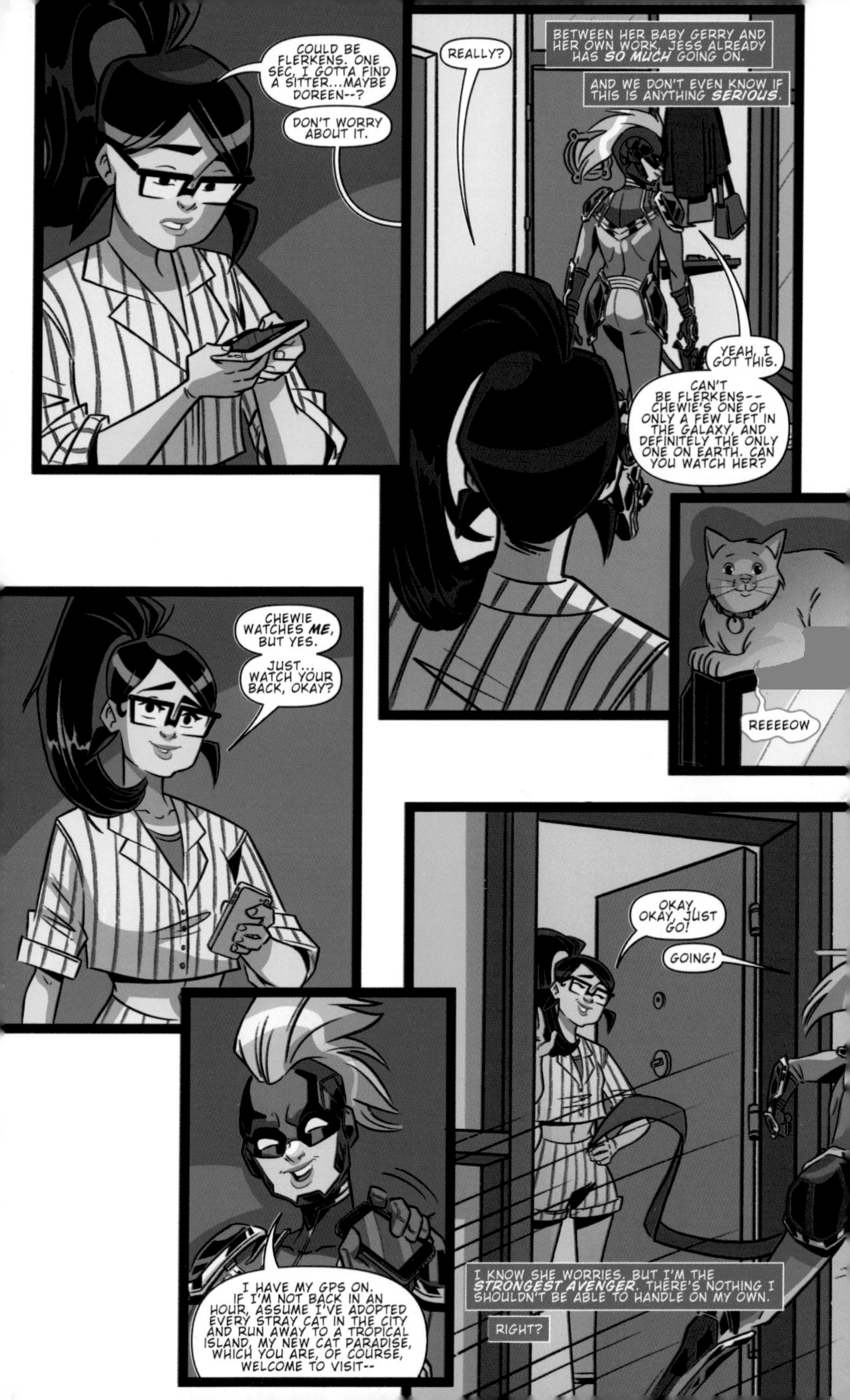
COULD BE FLERKENS. ONE SEC, I GOTTA FIND A SITTER...MAYBE DOREEN--?
DON'T WORRY ABOUT IT.
REALLY?
BETWEEN HER BABY GERRY AND HER OWN WORK, JESS ALREADY HAS SO MUCH GOING ON.
AND WE DON'T EVEN KNOW IF THIS IS ANYTHING SERIOUS.
YEAH, I GOT THIS.
CAN'T BE FLERKENS--CHEWIE'S ONE OF ONLY A FEW LEFT IN THE GALAXY, AND DEFINITELY THE ONLY ONE ON EARTH. CAN YOU WATCH HER?
REEEEOW
CHEWIE WATCHES ME, BUT YES.
JUST... WATCH YOUR BACK, OKAY?
I HAVE MY GPS ON. IF I'M NOT BACK IN AN HOUR, ASSUME I'VE ADOPTED EVERY STRAY CAT IN THE CITY AND RUN AWAY TO A TROPICAL ISLAND, MY NEW CAT PARADISE, WHICH YOU ARE, OF COURSE, WELCOME TO VISIT--
OKAY, OKAY, JUST GO!
GOING!
I KNOW SHE WORRIES. BUT I'M THE STRONGEST AVENGER. THERE'S NOTHING I SHOULDN'T BE ABLE TO HANDLE ON MY OWN.
RIGHT?

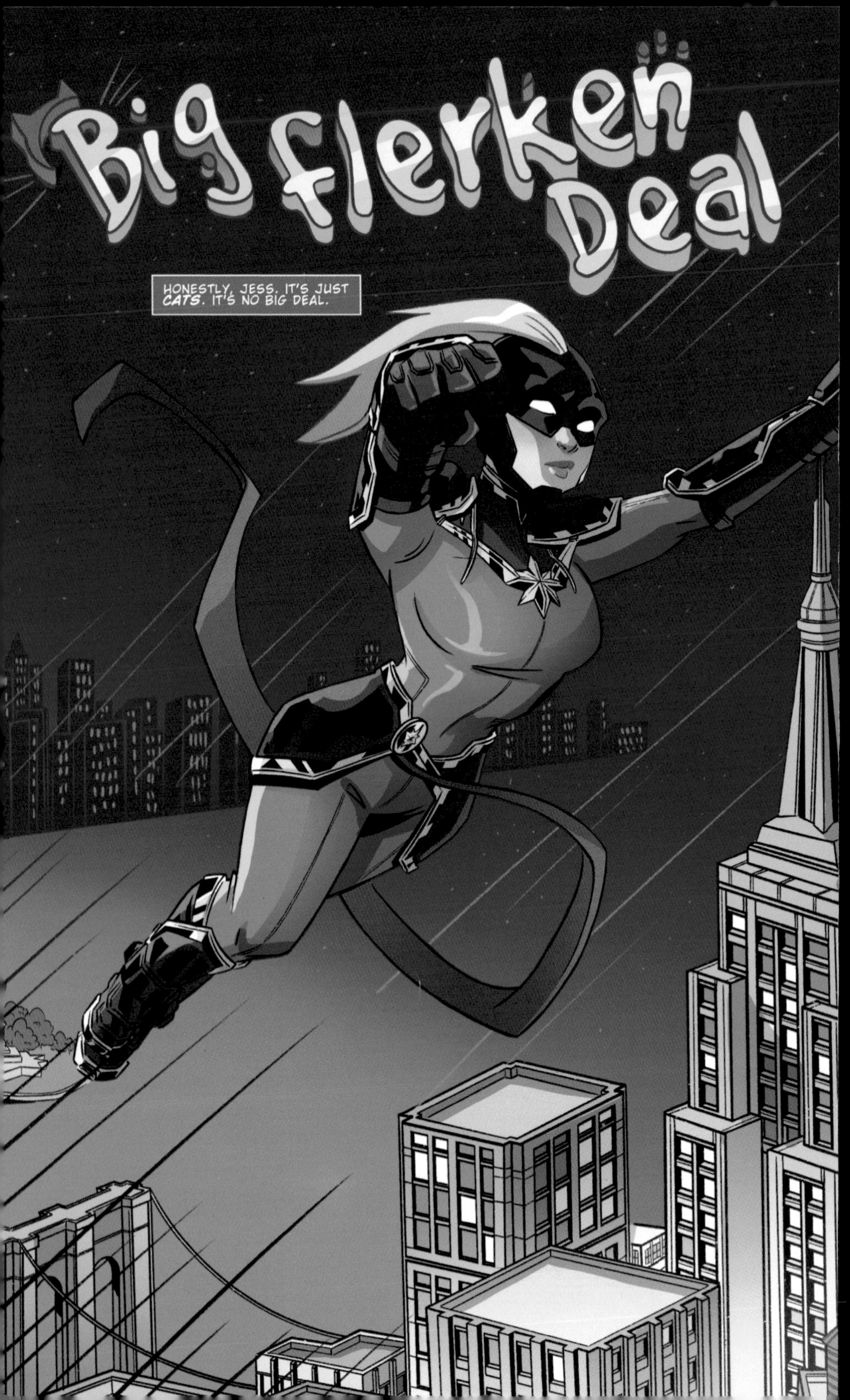
Big Flerken Deal
HONESTLY, JESS. IT'S JUST *CATS*. IT'S NO BIG DEAL.

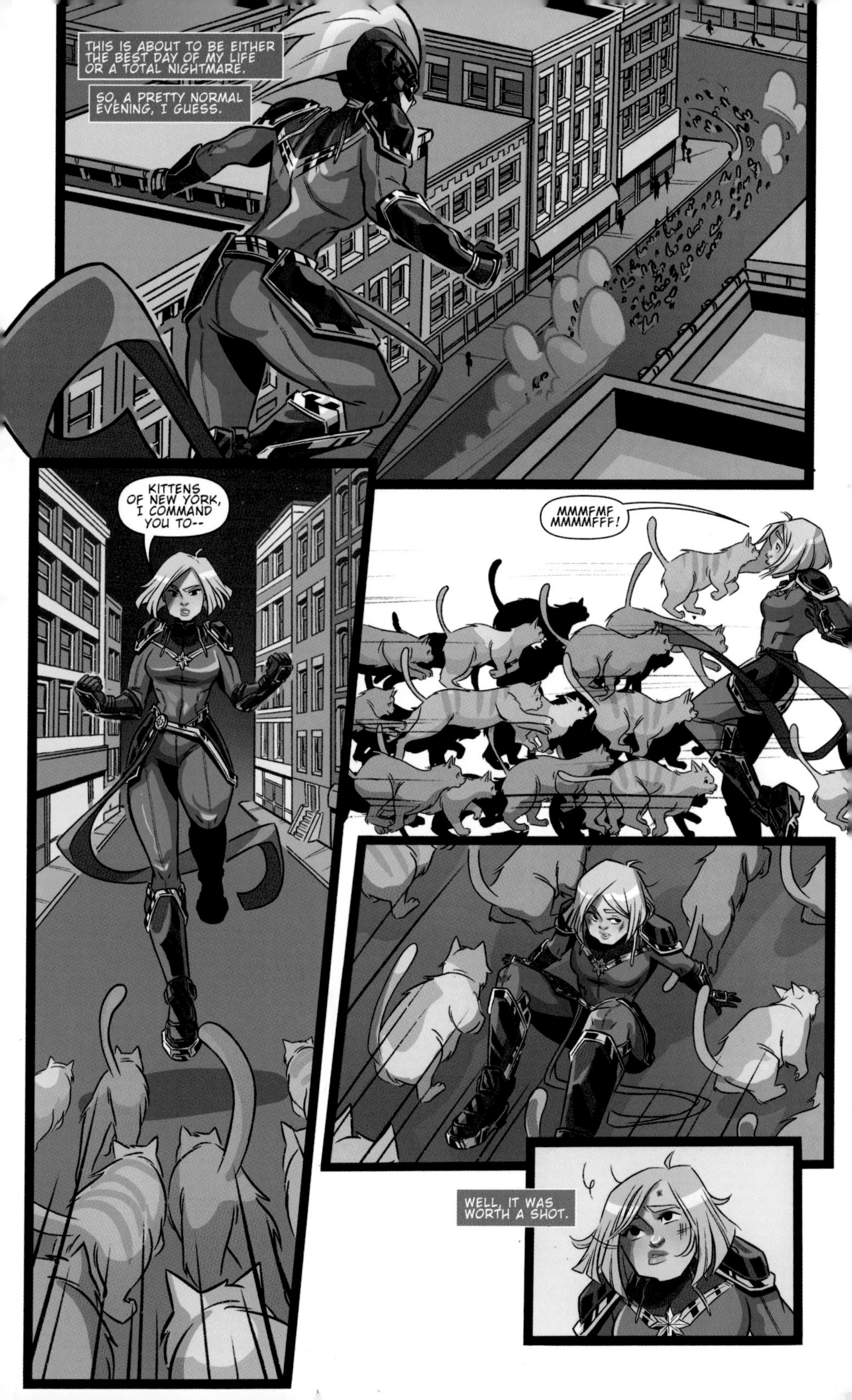
THIS IS ABOUT TO BE EITHER THE BEST DAY OF MY LIFE OR A TOTAL NIGHTMARE.
SO, A PRETTY NORMAL EVENING, I GUESS.
KITTENS OF NEW YORK, I COMMAND YOU TO--
MMMFMF MMMMFFF!
WELL, IT WAS WORTH A SHOT.

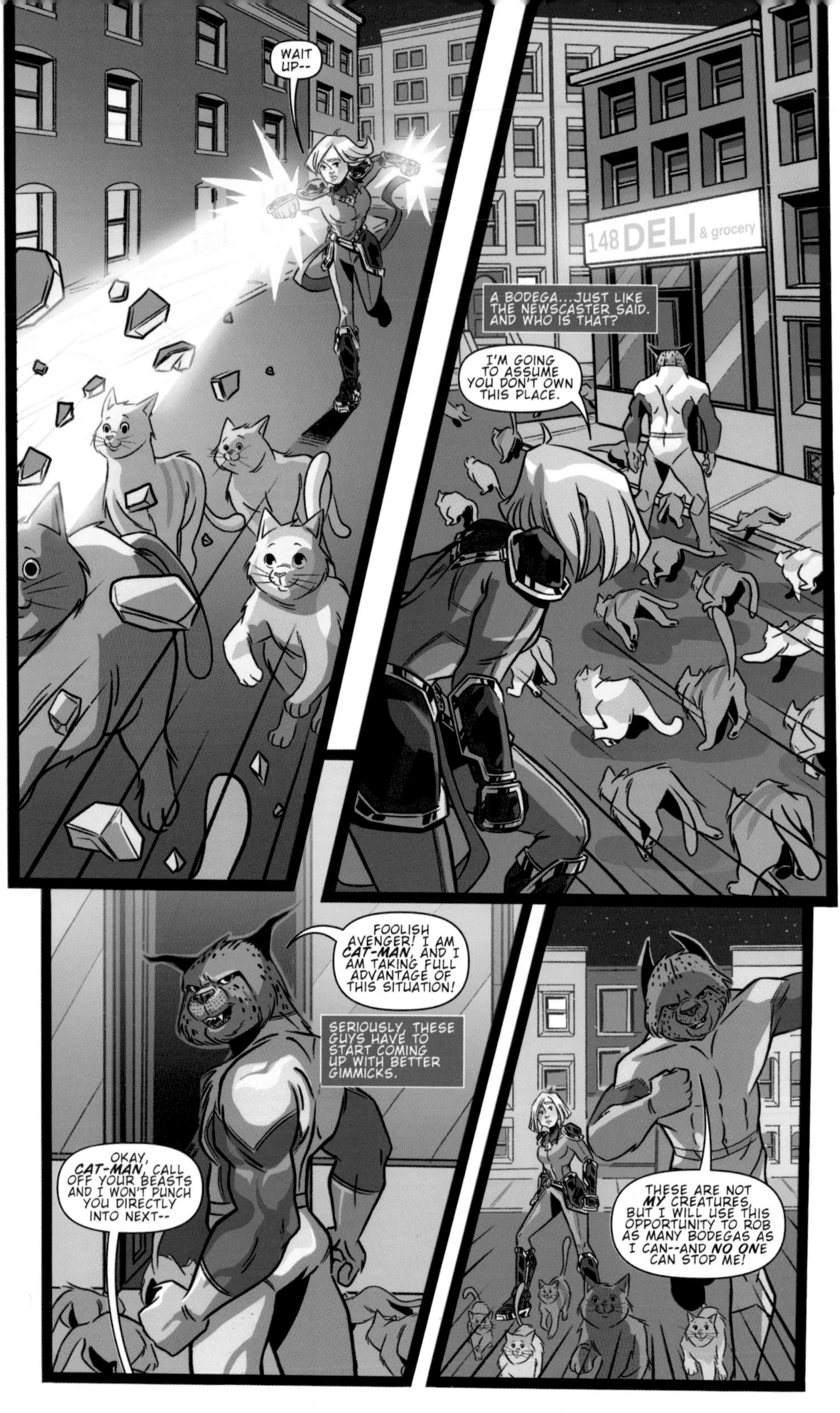
WAIT UP--
148 DELI & grocery
A BODEGA...JUST LIKE THE NEWSCASTER SAID. AND WHO IS THAT?
I'M GOING TO ASSUME YOU DON'T OWN THIS PLACE.
FOOLISH AVENGER! I AM CAT-MAN, AND I AM TAKING FULL ADVANTAGE OF THIS SITUATION!
SERIOUSLY, THESE GUYS HAVE TO START COMING UP WITH BETTER GIMMICKS.
OKAY, CAT-MAN, CALL OFF YOUR BEASTS AND I WON'T PUNCH YOU DIRECTLY INTO NEXT--
THESE ARE NOT MY CREATURES, BUT I WILL USE THIS OPPORTUNITY TO ROB AS MANY BODEGAS AS I CAN--AND NO ONE CAN STOP ME!

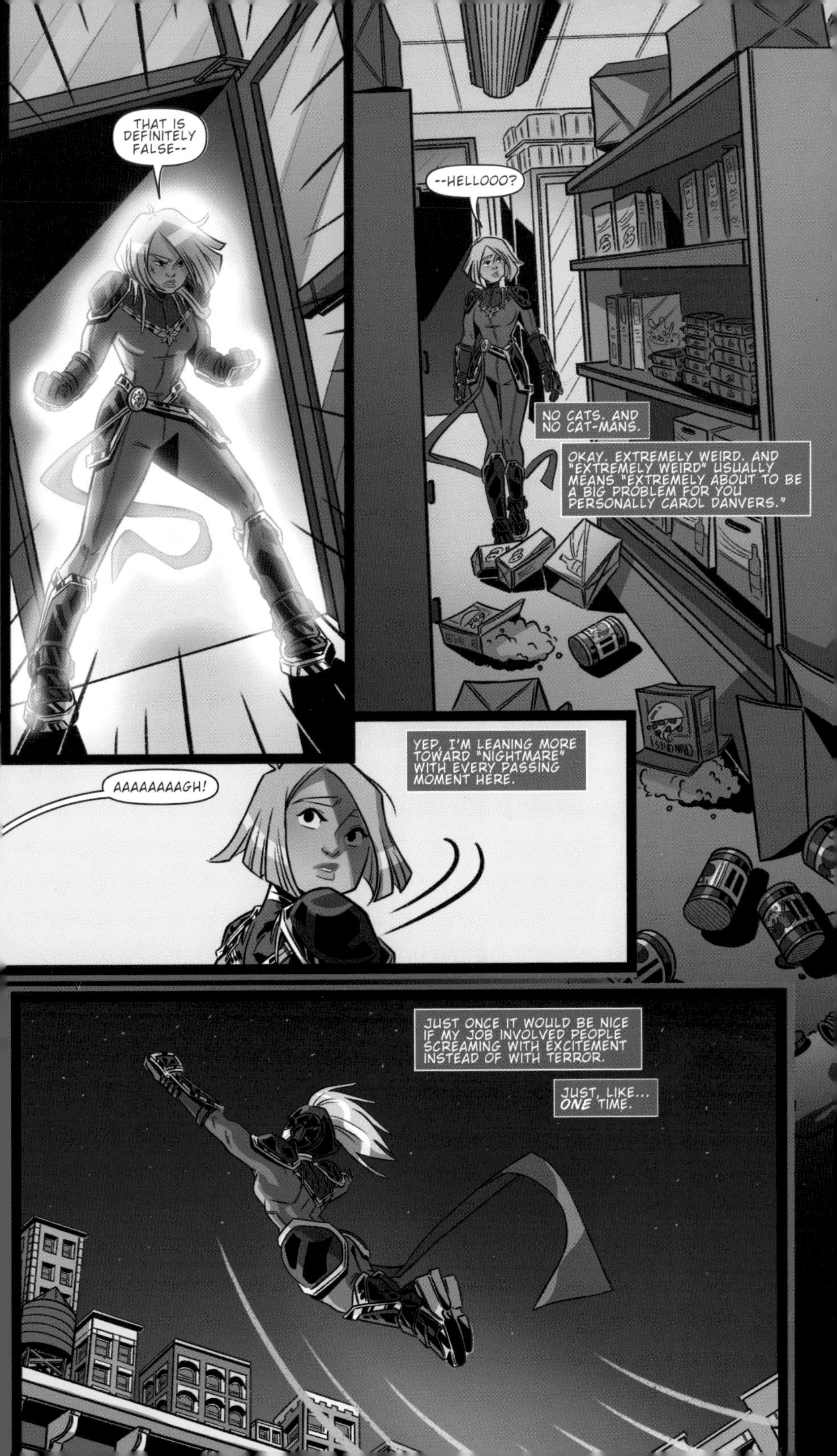

THAT IS DEFINITELY FALSE--
--HELLOOO?
NO CATS. AND NO CAT-MANS.
OKAY. EXTREMELY WEIRD. AND "EXTREMELY WEIRD" USUALLY MEANS "EXTREMELY ABOUT TO BE A BIG PROBLEM FOR YOU PERSONALLY CAROL DANVERS."
AAAAAAAAGH!
YEP, I'M LEANING MORE TOWARD "NIGHTMARE" WITH EVERY PASSING MOMENT HERE.
JUST ONCE IT WOULD BE NICE IF MY JOB INVOLVED PEOPLE SCREAMING WITH EXCITEMENT INSTEAD OF WITH TERROR.
JUST, LIKE... *ONE* TIME.

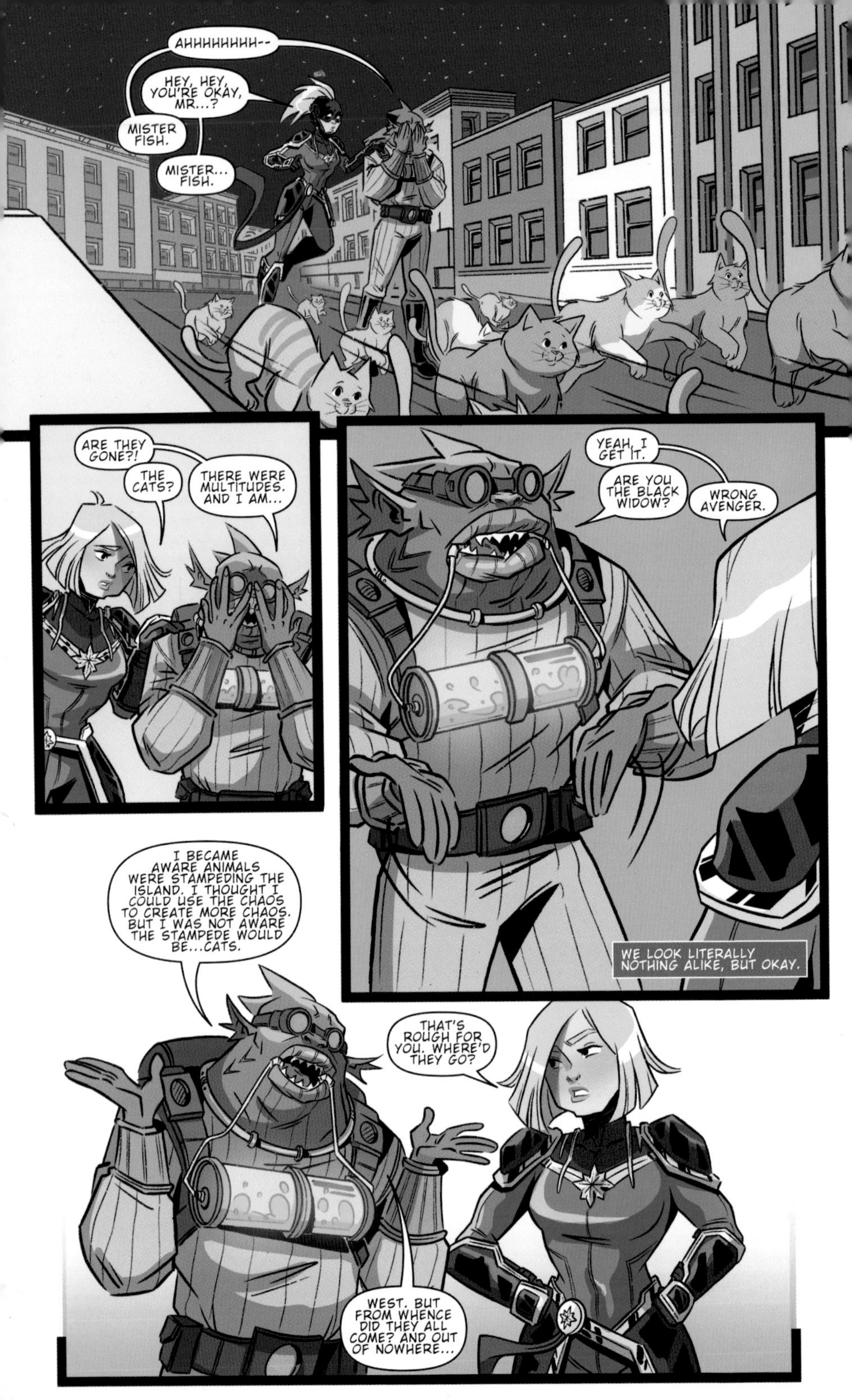
AHHHHHHHH--
HEY, HEY, YOU'RE OKAY, MR...?
MISTER FISH.
MISTER... FISH.
ARE THEY GONE?!
THE CATS?
THERE WERE MULTITUDES. AND I AM...
YEAH, I GET IT.
ARE YOU THE BLACK WIDOW?
WRONG AVENGER.
WE LOOK LITERALLY NOTHING ALIKE, BUT OKAY.
I BECAME AWARE ANIMALS WERE STAMPEDING THE ISLAND. I THOUGHT I COULD USE THE CHAOS TO CREATE MORE CHAOS. BUT I WAS NOT AWARE THE STAMPEDE WOULD BE...CATS.
THAT'S ROUGH FOR YOU. WHERE'D THEY GO?
WEST. BUT FROM WHENCE DID THEY ALL COME? AND OUT OF NOWHERE...

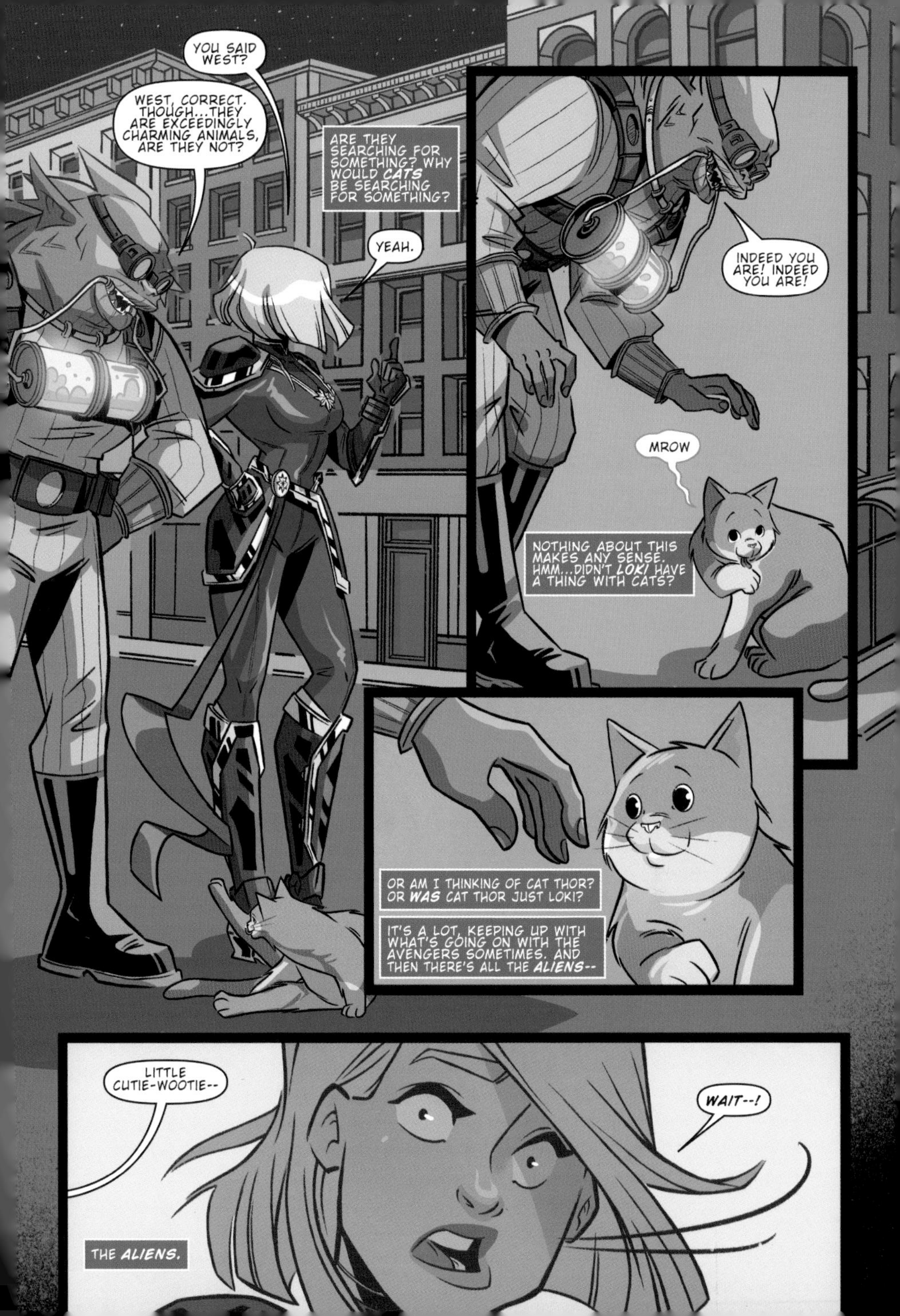
YOU SAID WEST?
WEST, CORRECT. THOUGH...THEY ARE EXCEEDINGLY CHARMING ANIMALS, ARE THEY NOT?
ARE THEY SEARCHING FOR SOMETHING? WHY WOULD CATS BE SEARCHING FOR SOMETHING?
YEAH.
INDEED YOU ARE! INDEED YOU ARE!
MROW
NOTHING ABOUT THIS MAKES ANY SENSE. HMM...DIDN'T LOKI HAVE A THING WITH CATS?
OR AM I THINKING OF CAT THOR? OR WAS CAT THOR JUST LOKI?
IT'S A LOT, KEEPING UP WITH WHAT'S GOING ON WITH THE AVENGERS SOMETIMES. AND THEN THERE'S ALL THE ALIENS--
LITTLE CUTIE-WOOTIE--
WAIT--!
THE ALIENS.

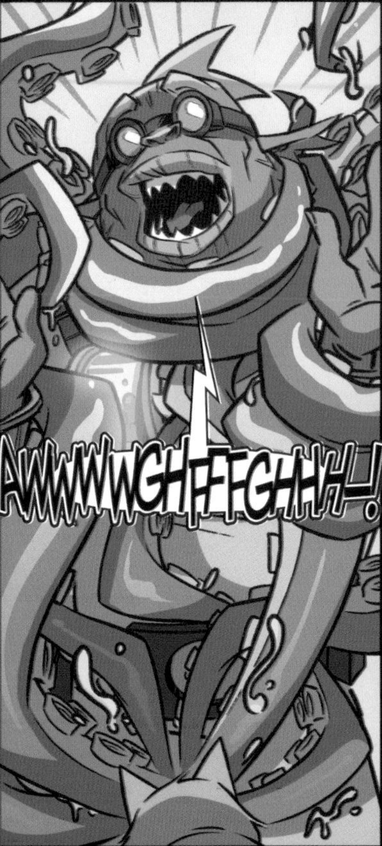
AWWWWGHFFGHHH—!

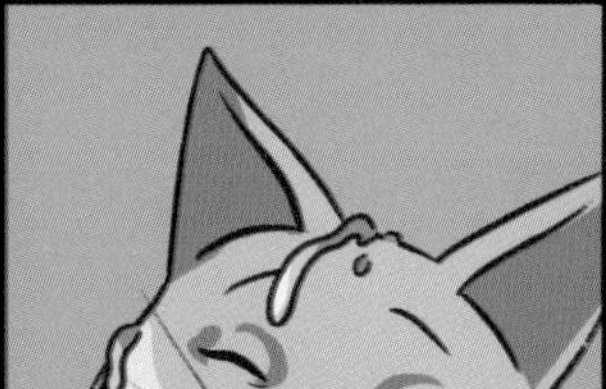

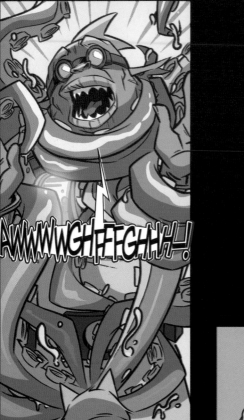

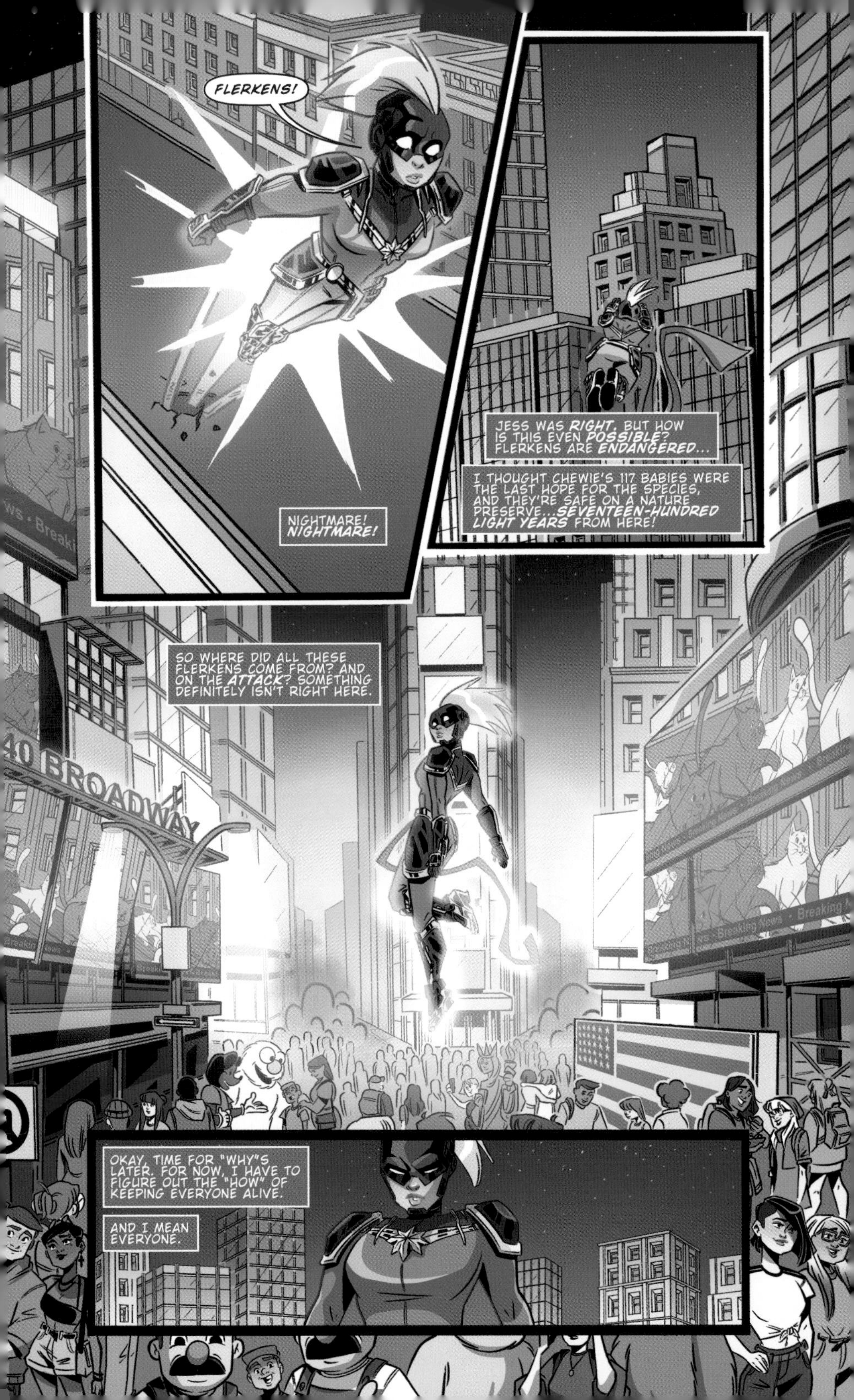
FLERKENS!
NIGHTMARE! NIGHTMARE!
JESS WAS RIGHT. BUT HOW IS THIS EVEN POSSIBLE? FLERKENS ARE ENDANGERED...
I THOUGHT CHEWIE'S 117 BABIES WERE THE LAST HOPE FOR THE SPECIES, AND THEY'RE SAFE ON A NATURE PRESERVE...SEVENTEEN-HUNDRED LIGHT YEARS FROM HERE!
SO WHERE DID ALL THESE FLERKENS COME FROM? AND ON THE ATTACK? SOMETHING DEFINITELY ISN'T RIGHT HERE.
40 BROADWAY
Breaking News
OKAY, TIME FOR "WHY"'S LATER. FOR NOW, I HAVE TO FIGURE OUT THE "HOW" OF KEEPING EVERYONE ALIVE.
AND I MEAN EVERYONE.

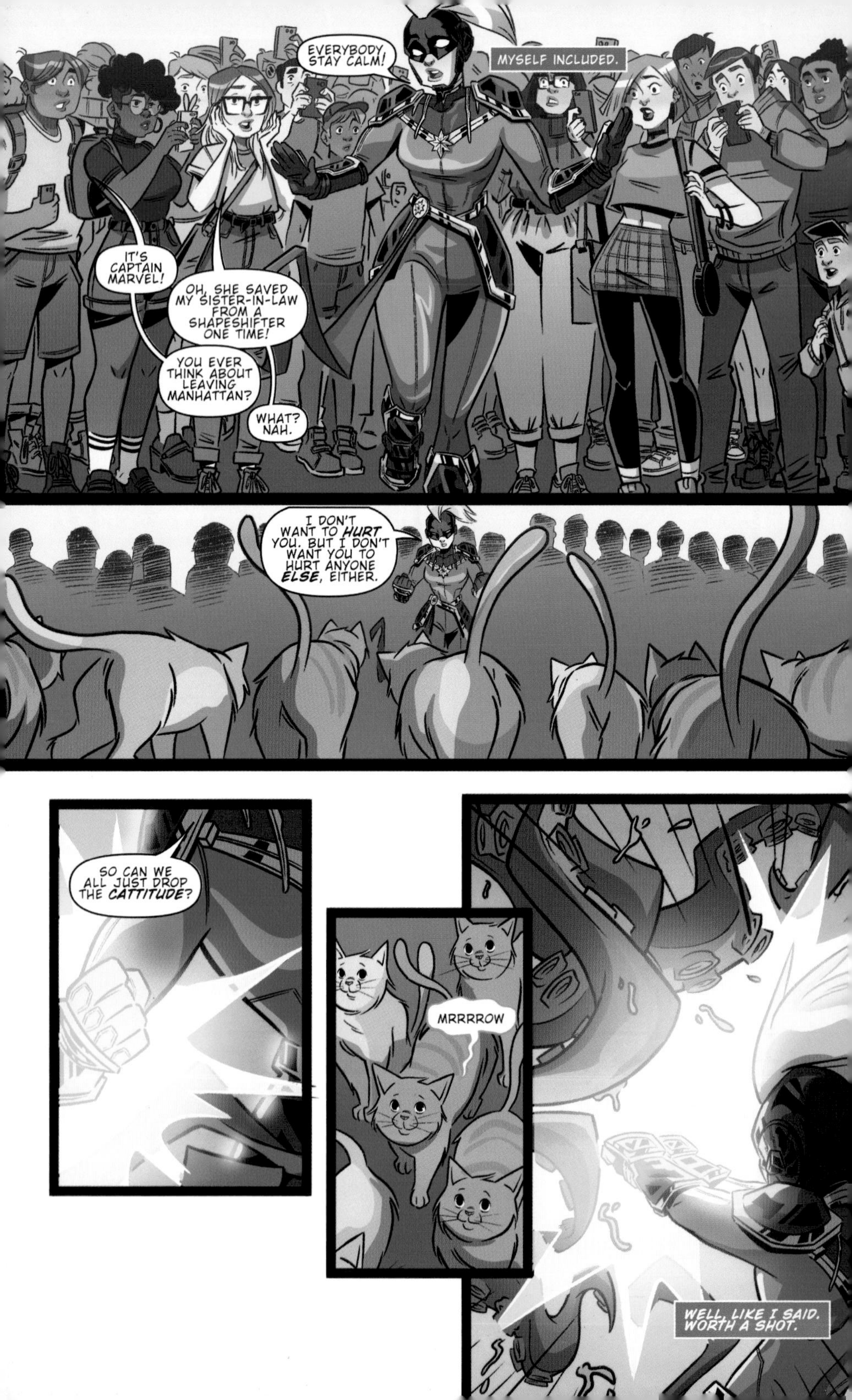
EVERYBODY STAY CALM!
MYSELF INCLUDED.
IT'S CAPTAIN MARVEL!
OH, SHE SAVED MY SISTER-IN-LAW FROM A SHAPESHIFTER ONE TIME!
YOU EVER THINK ABOUT LEAVING MANHATTAN?
WHAT? NAH.
I DON'T WANT TO HURT YOU. BUT I DON'T WANT YOU TO HURT ANYONE ELSE, EITHER.
SO CAN WE ALL JUST DROP THE CATTITUDE?
MRRRROW
WELL, LIKE I SAID. WORTH A SHOT.

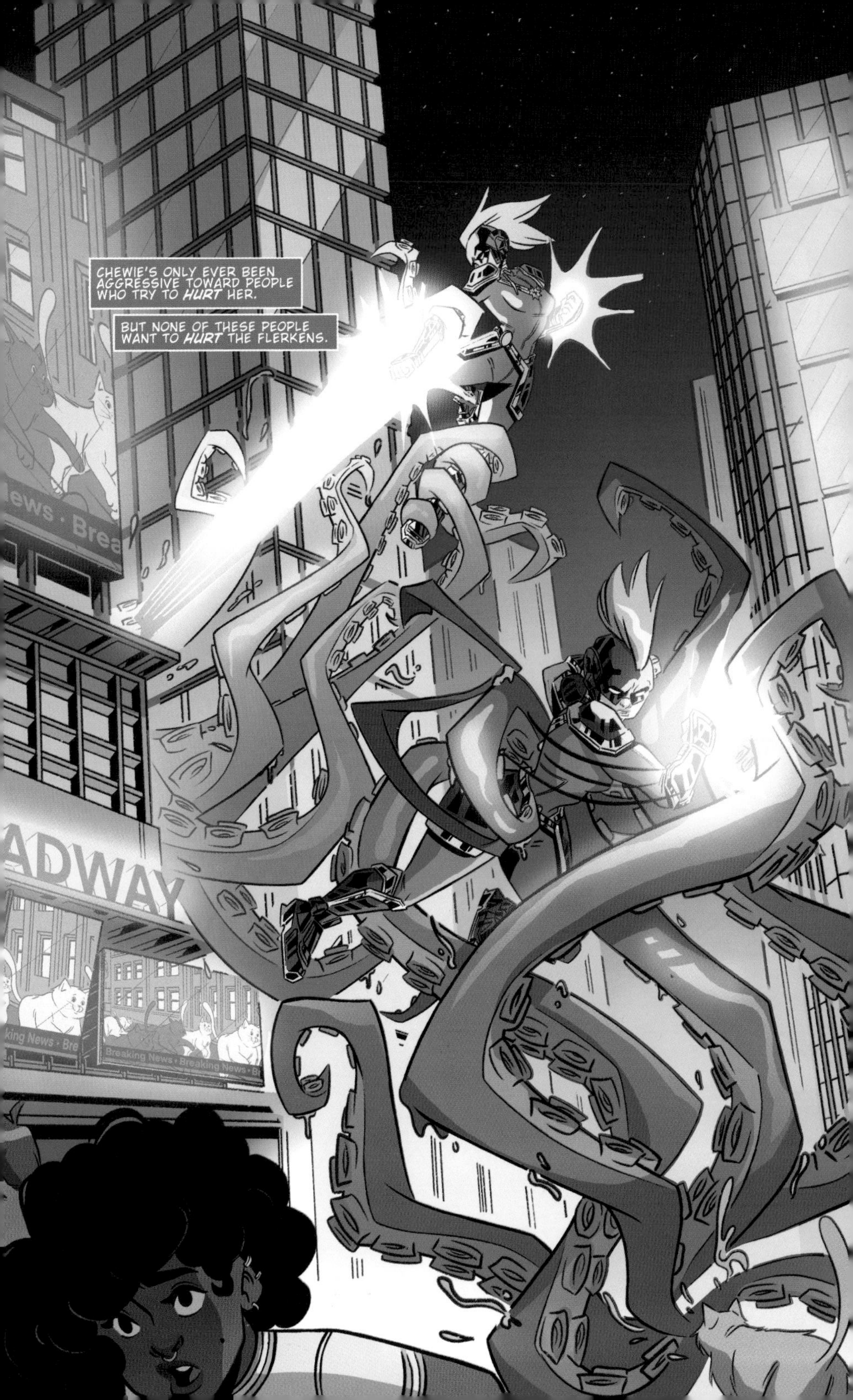
CHEWIE'S ONLY EVER BEEN AGGRESSIVE TOWARD PEOPLE WHO TRY TO *HURT* HER.
BUT NONE OF THESE PEOPLE WANT TO *HURT* THE FLERKENS.
ADWAY
Breaking News · Breaking News

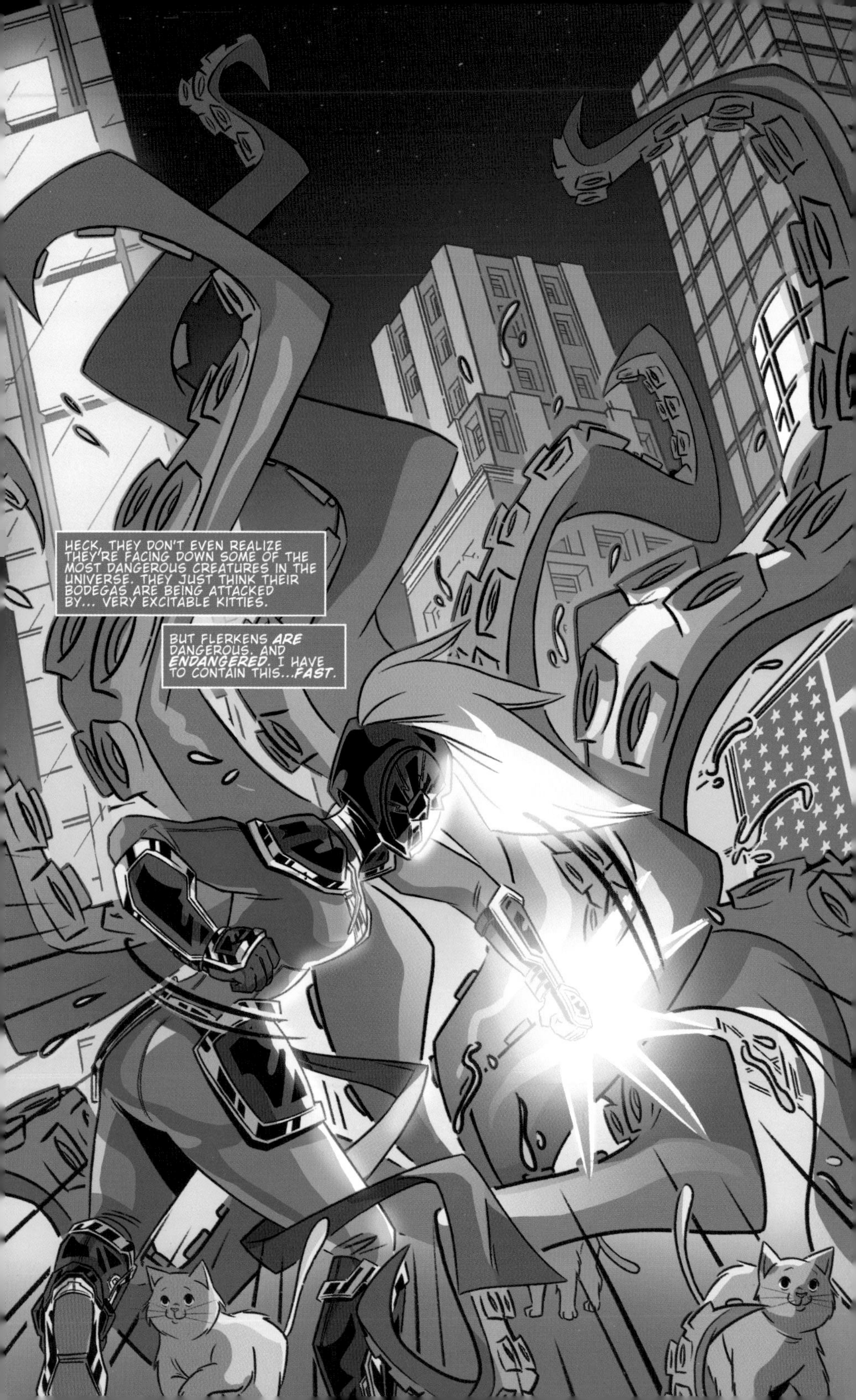
HECK, THEY DON'T EVEN REALIZE THEY'RE FACING DOWN SOME OF THE MOST DANGEROUS CREATURES IN THE UNIVERSE. THEY JUST THINK THEIR BODEGAS ARE BEING ATTACKED BY... VERY EXCITABLE KITTIES.
BUT FLERKENS *ARE* DANGEROUS. AND *ENDANGERED*. I HAVE TO CONTAIN THIS...*FAST*.

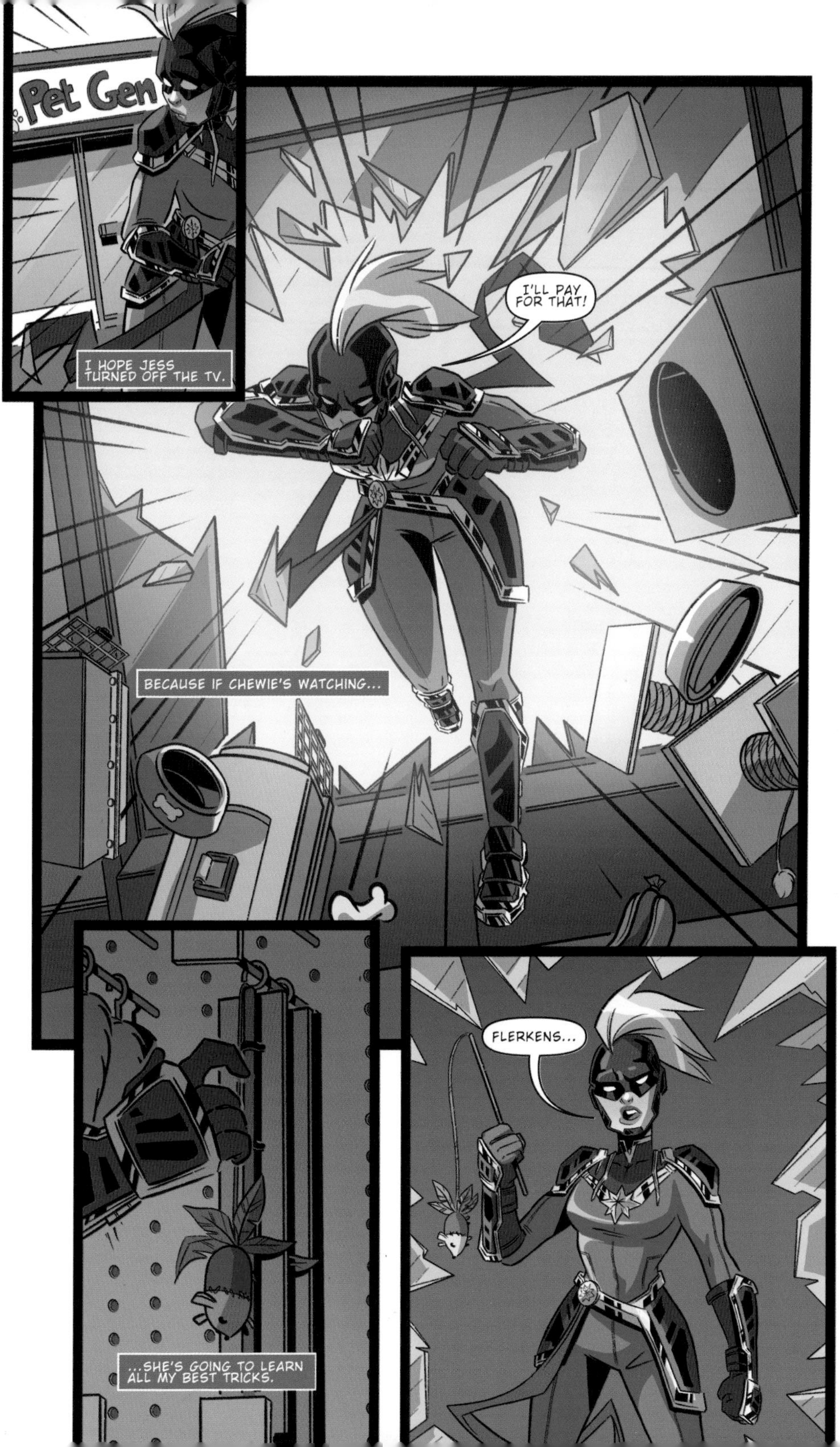
Pet Gen
I HOPE JESS TURNED OFF THE TV.
I'LL PAY FOR THAT!
BECAUSE IF CHEWIE'S WATCHING...
...SHE'S GOING TO LEARN ALL MY BEST TRICKS.
FLERKENS...

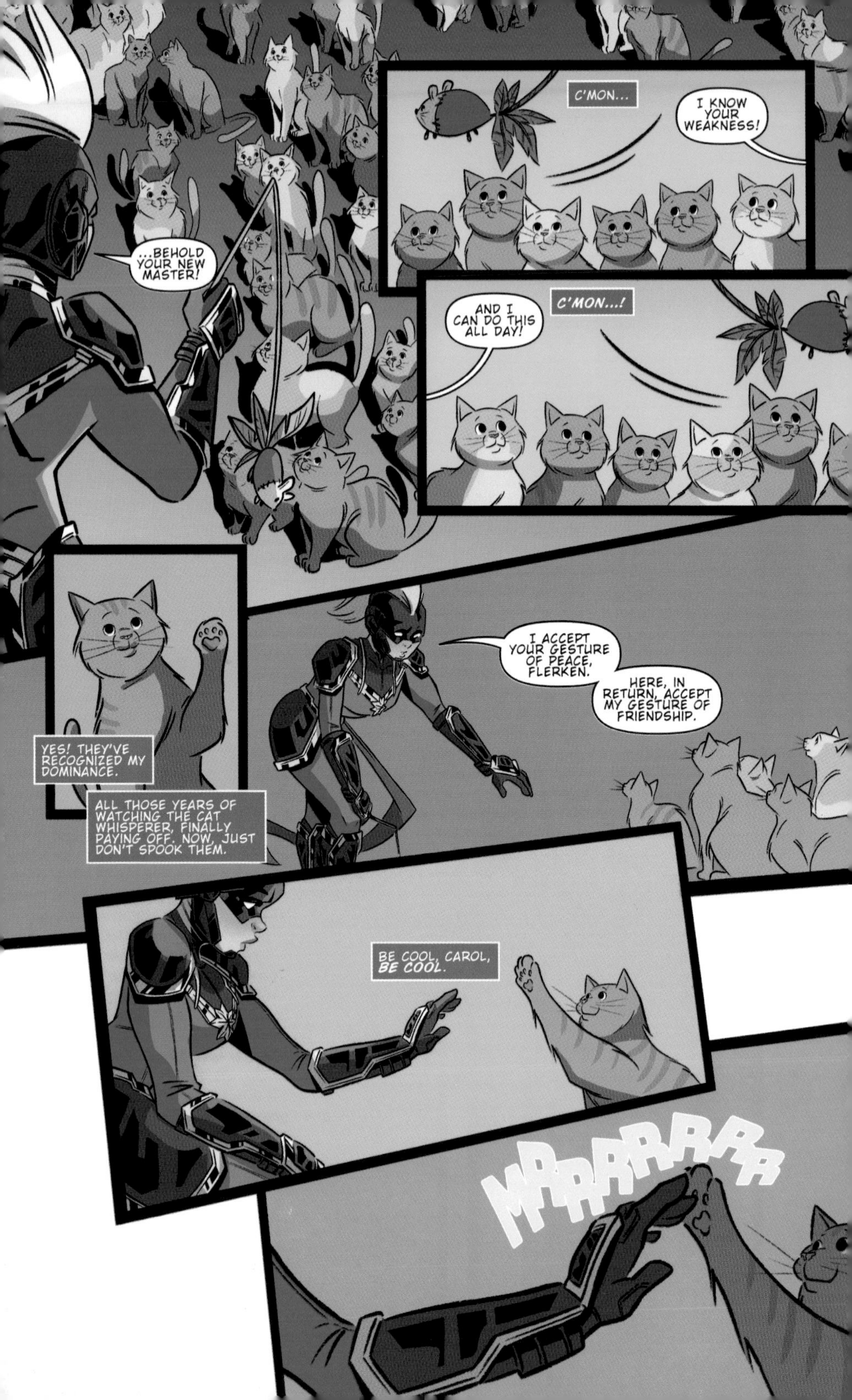
...BEHOLD YOUR NEW MASTER!
C'MON...
I KNOW YOUR WEAKNESS!
C'MON...!
AND I CAN DO THIS ALL DAY!
YES! THEY'VE RECOGNIZED MY DOMINANCE.
ALL THOSE YEARS OF WATCHING THE CAT WHISPERER, FINALLY PAYING OFF. NOW, JUST DON'T SPOOK THEM.
I ACCEPT YOUR GESTURE OF PEACE, FLERKEN.
HERE, IN RETURN, ACCEPT MY GESTURE OF FRIENDSHIP.
BE COOL, CAROL, *BE COOL*.
MRRRRRRRR

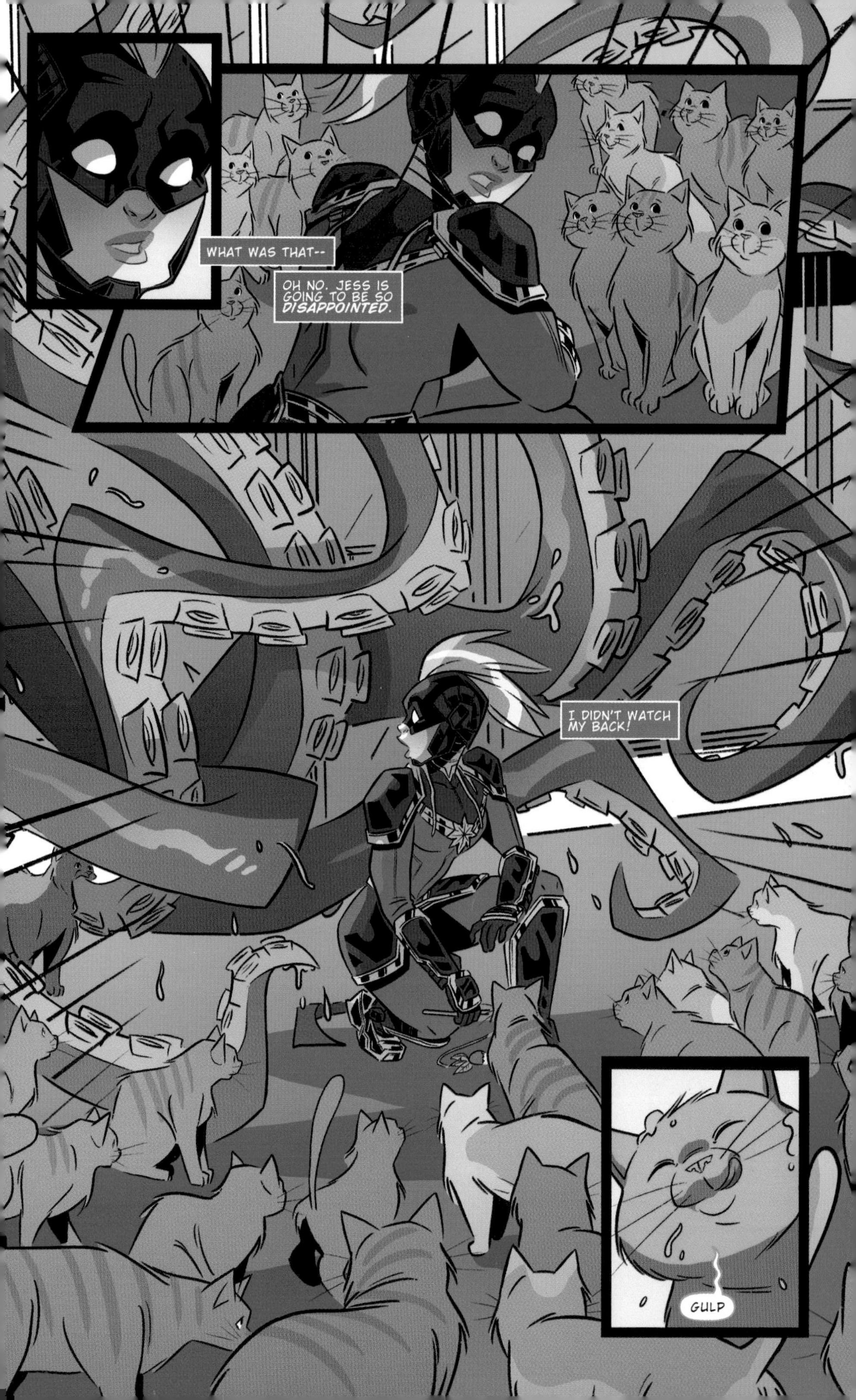
WHAT WAS THAT--
OH NO. JESS IS GOING TO BE SO DISAPPOINTED.
I DIDN'T WATCH MY BACK!
GULP

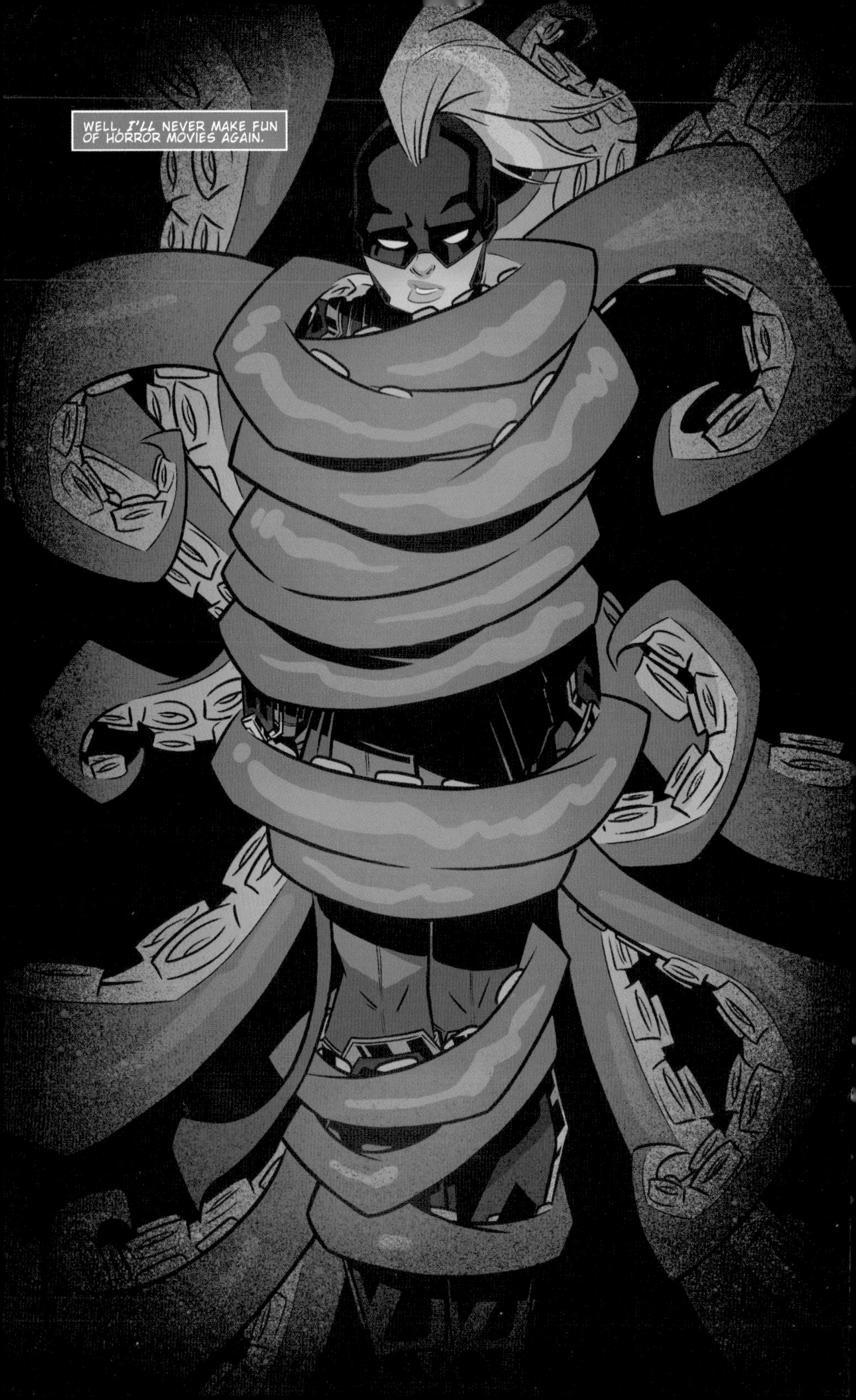
WELL, I'LL NEVER MAKE FUN OF HORROR MOVIES AGAIN.

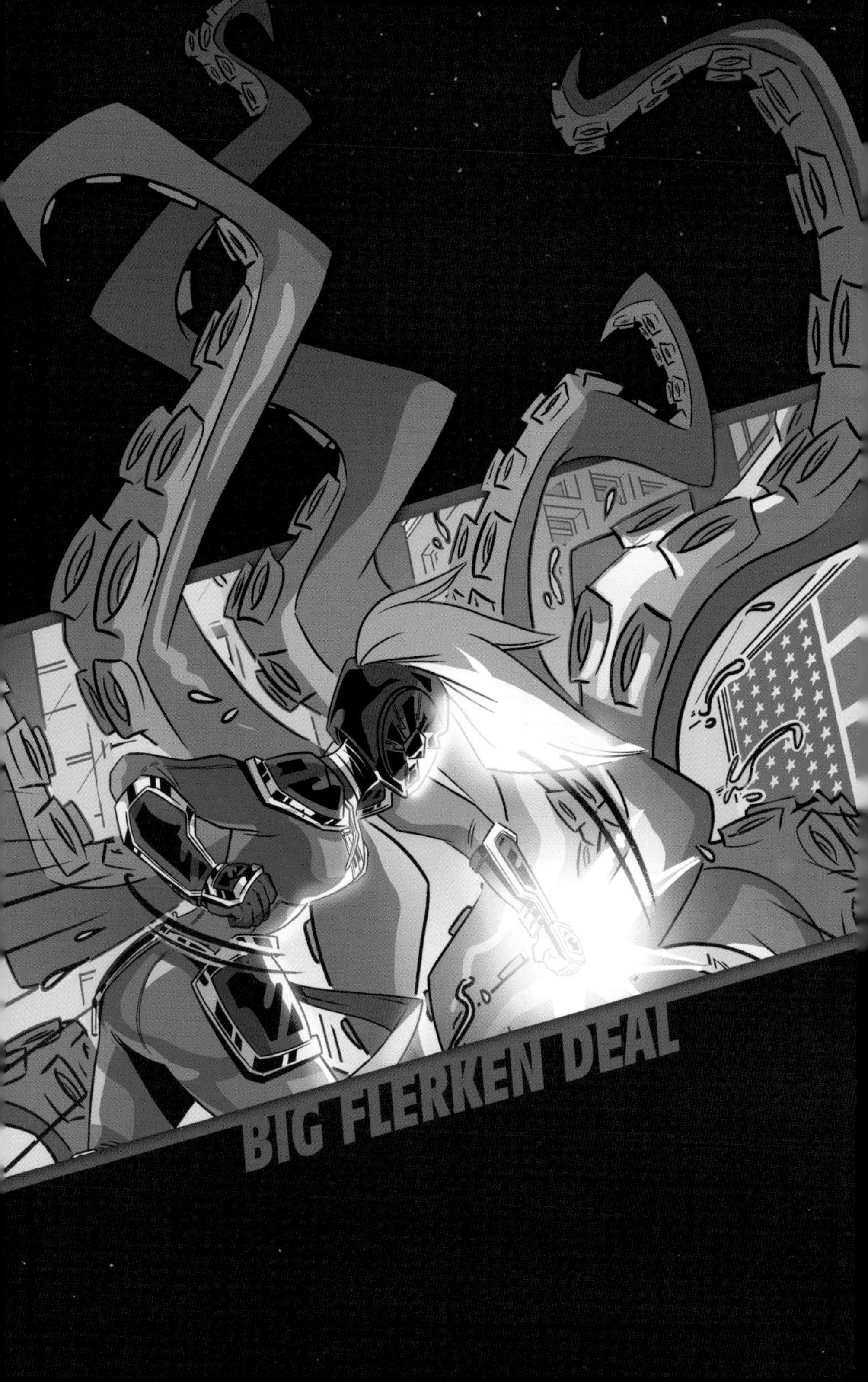
BIG FLERKEN DEAL

ART BY: SWEENEY BOO

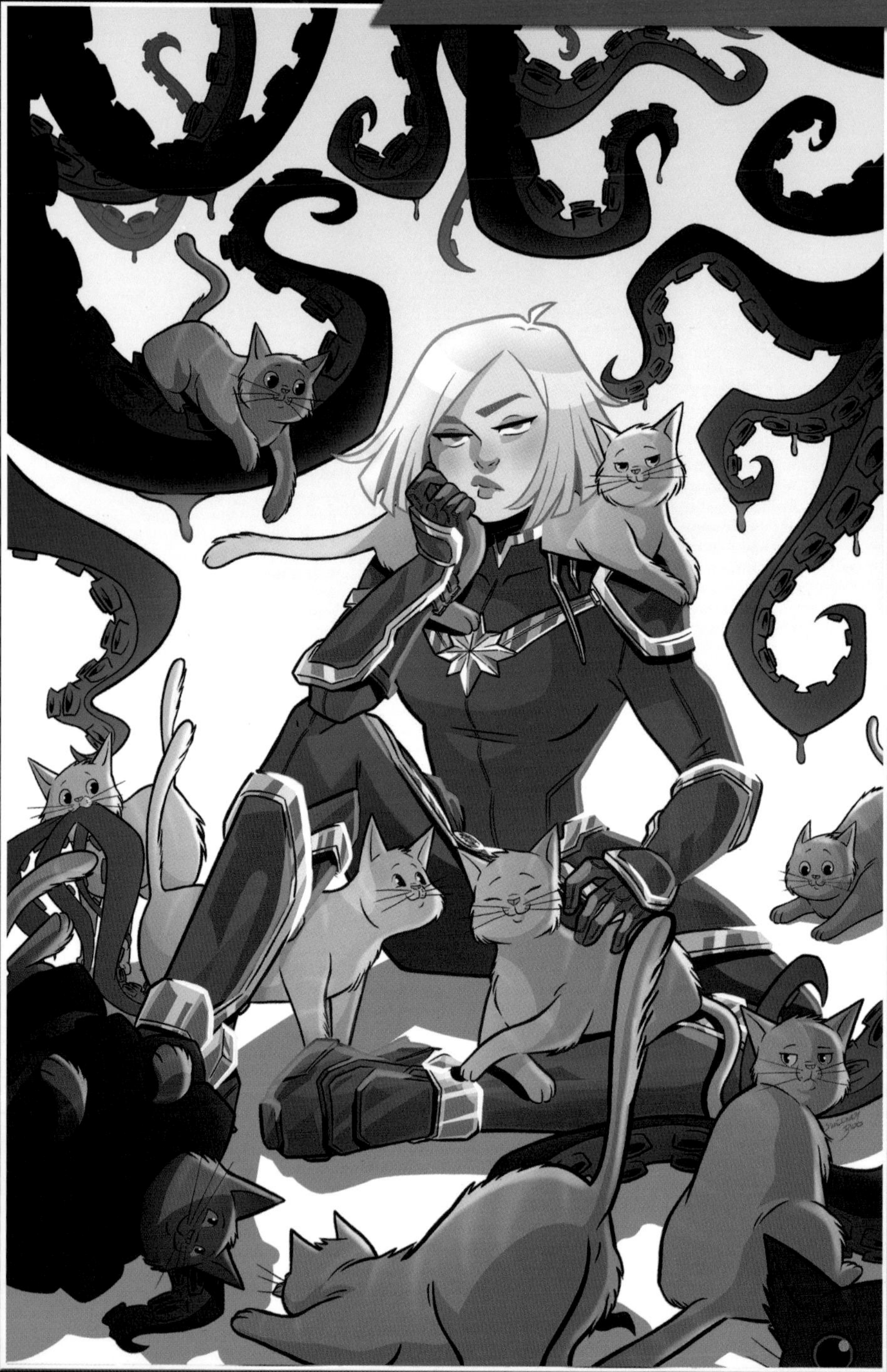

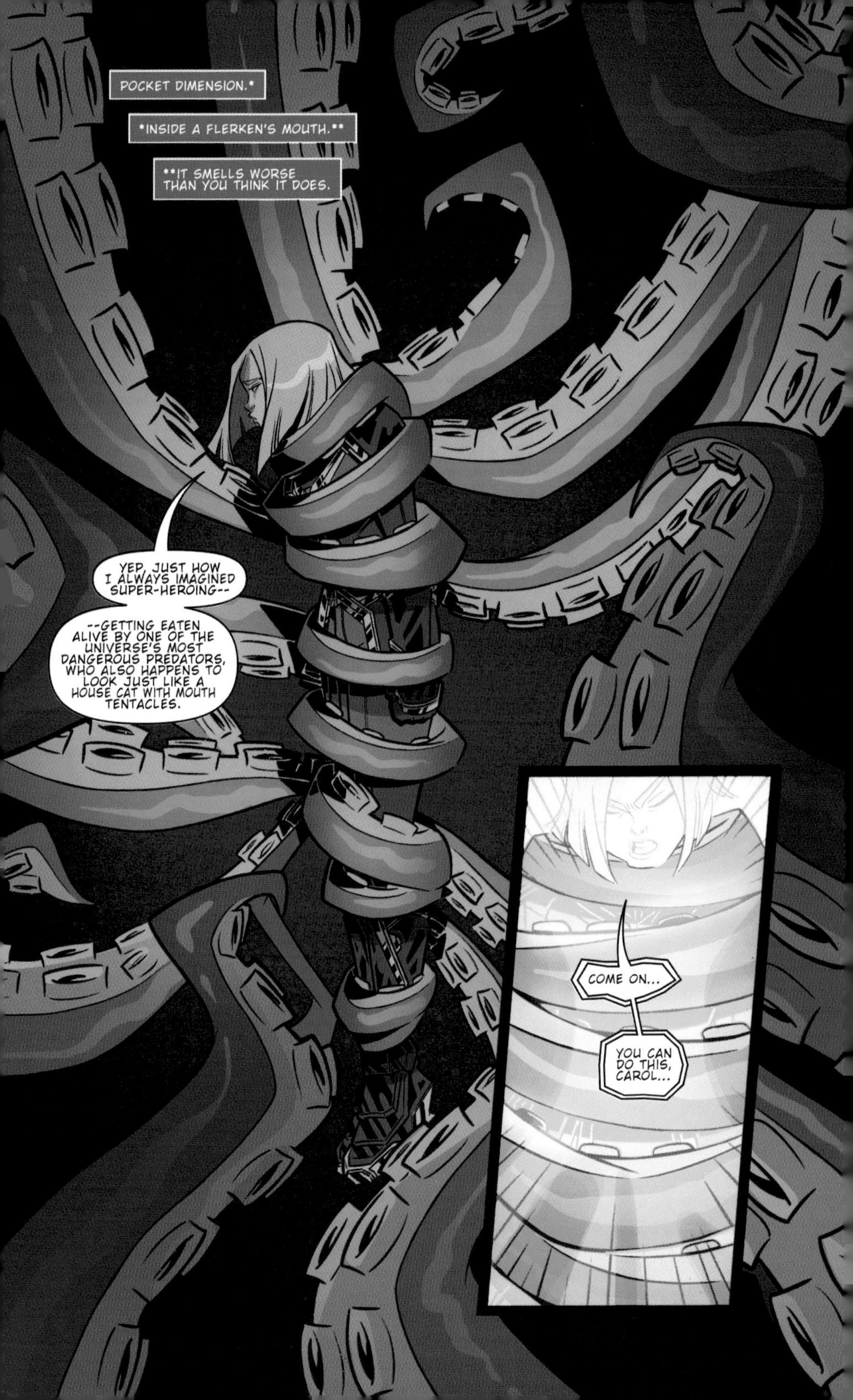
POCKET DIMENSION.*
*INSIDE A FLERKEN'S MOUTH.**
**IT SMELLS WORSE THAN YOU THINK IT DOES.
YEP, JUST HOW I ALWAYS IMAGINED SUPER-HEROING--
--GETTING EATEN ALIVE BY ONE OF THE UNIVERSE'S MOST DANGEROUS PREDATORS, WHO ALSO HAPPENS TO LOOK JUST LIKE A HOUSE CAT WITH MOUTH TENTACLES.
COME ON...
YOU CAN DO THIS, CAROL...

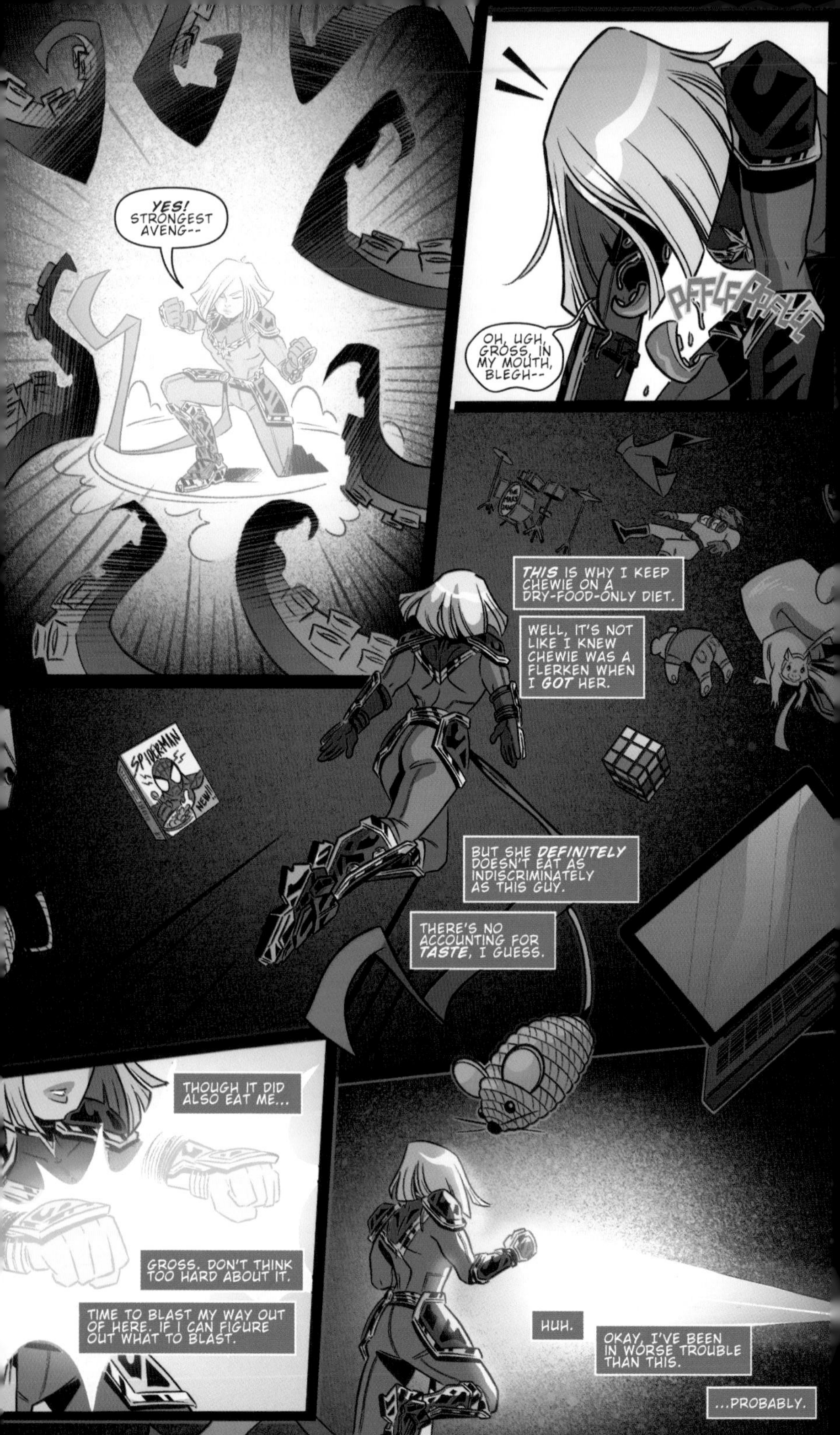
YES! STRONGEST AVENG--
PFFLFPFFL
OH, UGH, GROSS, IN MY MOUTH, BLEGH--
THIS IS WHY I KEEP CHEWIE ON A DRY-FOOD-ONLY DIET.
WELL, IT'S NOT LIKE I KNEW CHEWIE WAS A FLERKEN WHEN I GOT HER.
SPIDERMAN
NEW!!
BUT SHE DEFINITELY DOESN'T EAT AS INDISCRIMINATELY AS THIS GUY.
THERE'S NO ACCOUNTING FOR TASTE, I GUESS.
THOUGH IT DID ALSO EAT ME...
GROSS. DON'T THINK TOO HARD ABOUT IT.
TIME TO BLAST MY WAY OUT OF HERE. IF I CAN FIGURE OUT WHAT TO BLAST.
HUH.
OKAY, I'VE BEEN IN WORSE TROUBLE THAN THIS.
...PROBABLY.

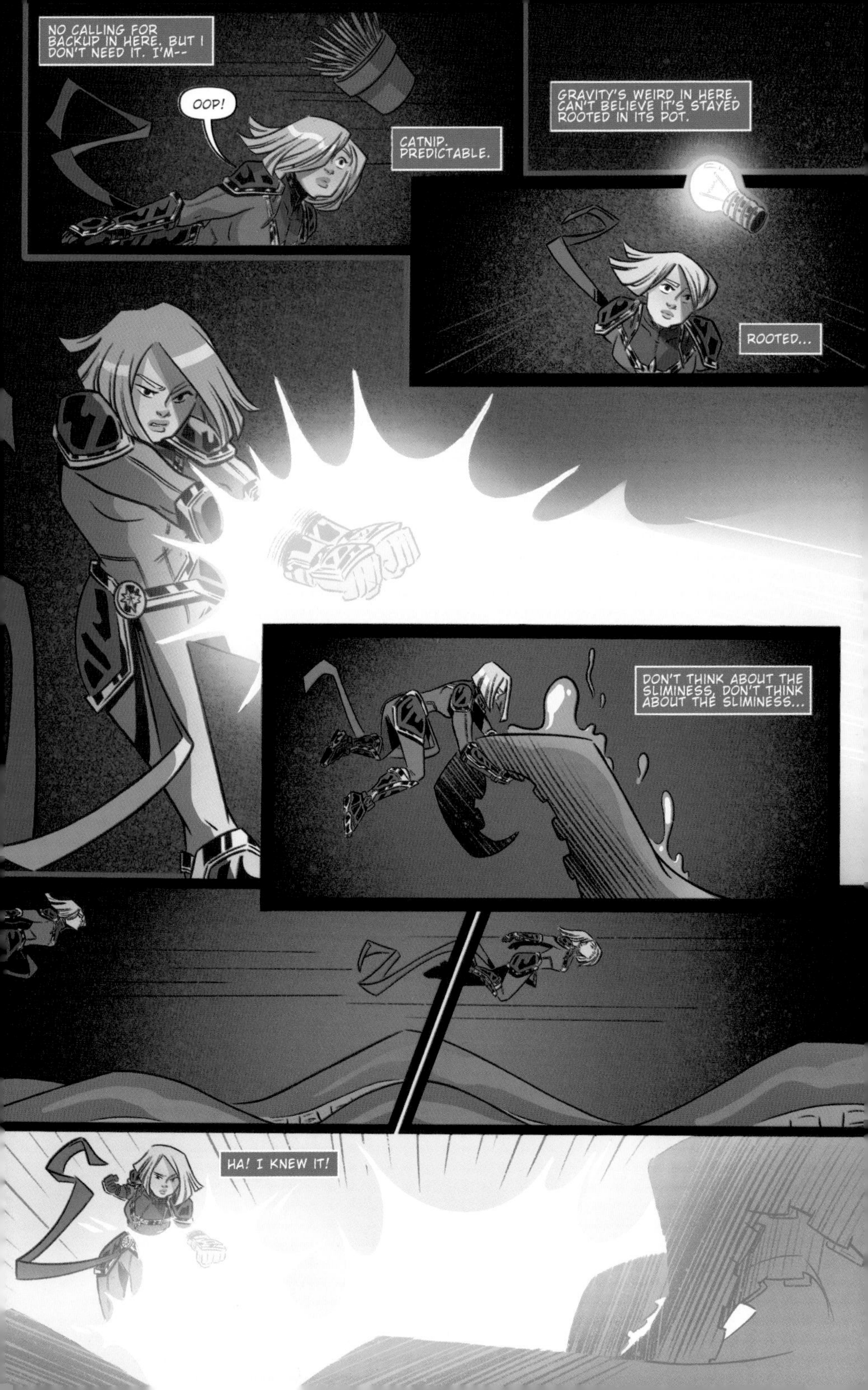
NO CALLING FOR BACKUP IN HERE. BUT I DON'T NEED IT. I'M--
OOP!
CATNIP. PREDICTABLE.
GRAVITY'S WEIRD IN HERE. CAN'T BELIEVE IT'S STAYED ROOTED IN ITS POT.
ROOTED...
DON'T THINK ABOUT THE SLIMINESS, DON'T THINK ABOUT THE SLIMINESS...
HA! I KNEW IT!

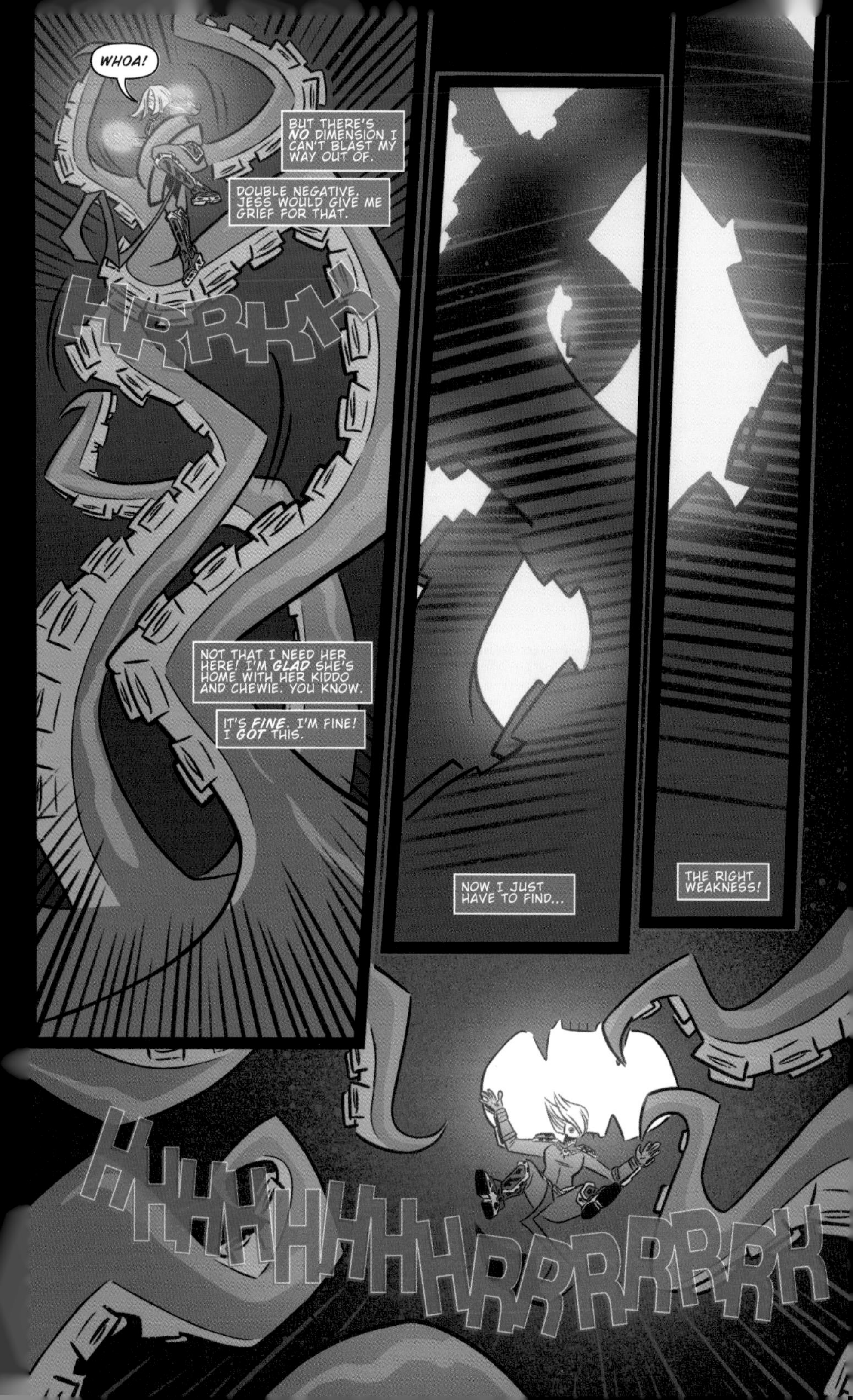
WHOA!
BUT THERE'S *NO* DIMENSION I CAN'T BLAST MY WAY OUT OF.
DOUBLE NEGATIVE. JESS WOULD GIVE ME GRIEF FOR THAT.
NOT THAT I NEED HER HERE! I'M *GLAD* SHE'S HOME WITH HER KIDDO AND CHEWIE. YOU KNOW.
IT'S *FINE*. I'M FINE! I *GOT* THIS.
NOW I JUST HAVE TO FIND...
THE RIGHT WEAKNESS!

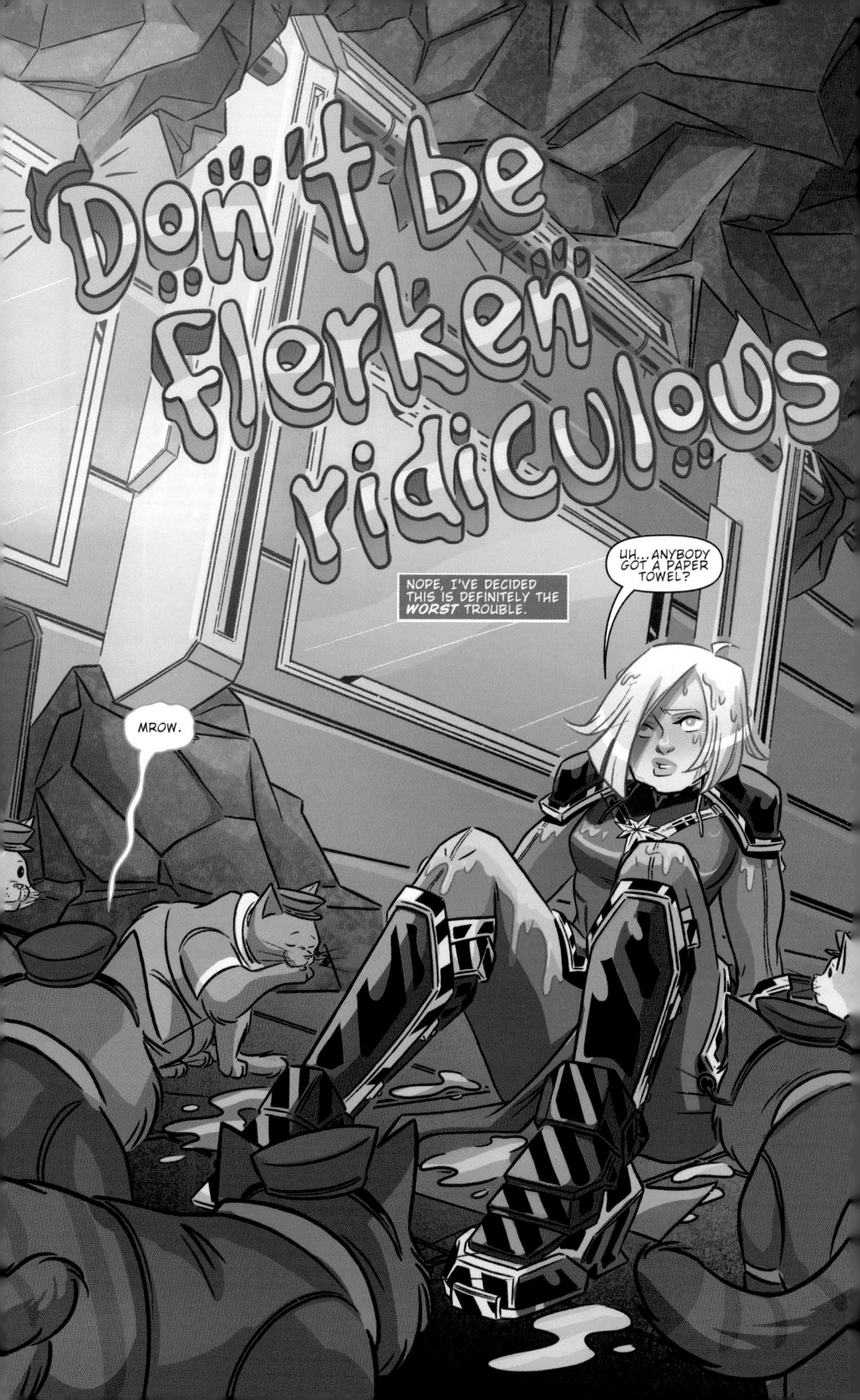
Don't be flerken ridiculous
NOPE, I'VE DECIDED THIS IS DEFINITELY THE WORST TROUBLE.
UH...ANYBODY GOT A PAPER TOWEL?
MROW.

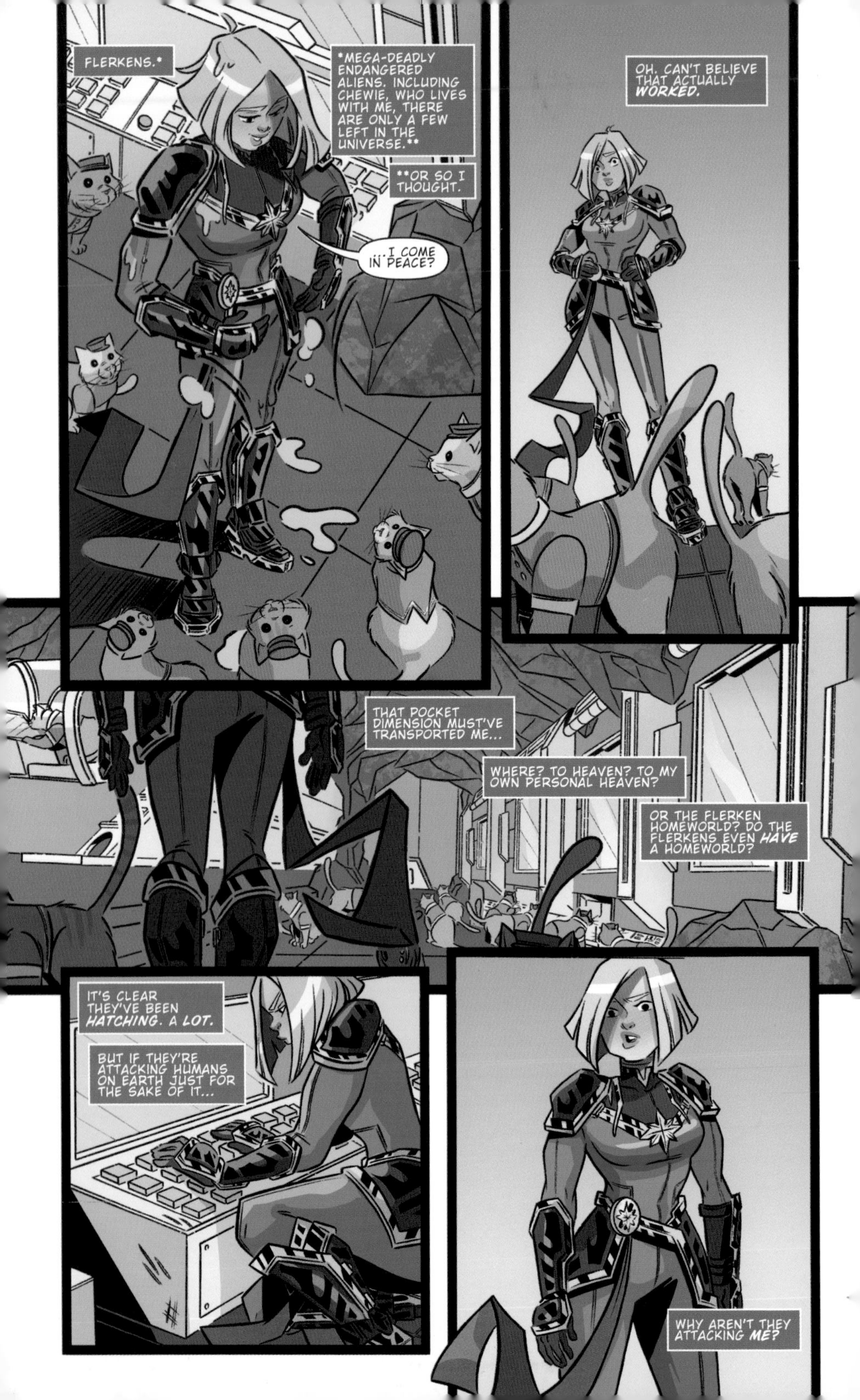
FLERKENS.*
*MEGA-DEADLY ENDANGERED ALIENS. INCLUDING CHEWIE, WHO LIVES WITH ME, THERE ARE ONLY A FEW LEFT IN THE UNIVERSE.**
**OR SO I THOUGHT.
...I COME IN PEACE?
OH. CAN'T BELIEVE THAT ACTUALLY WORKED.
THAT POCKET DIMENSION MUST'VE TRANSPORTED ME...
WHERE? TO HEAVEN? TO MY OWN PERSONAL HEAVEN?
OR THE FLERKEN HOMEWORLD? DO THE FLERKENS EVEN HAVE A HOMEWORLD?
IT'S CLEAR THEY'VE BEEN HATCHING. A LOT.
BUT IF THEY'RE ATTACKING HUMANS ON EARTH JUST FOR THE SAKE OF IT...
WHY AREN'T THEY ATTACKING ME?

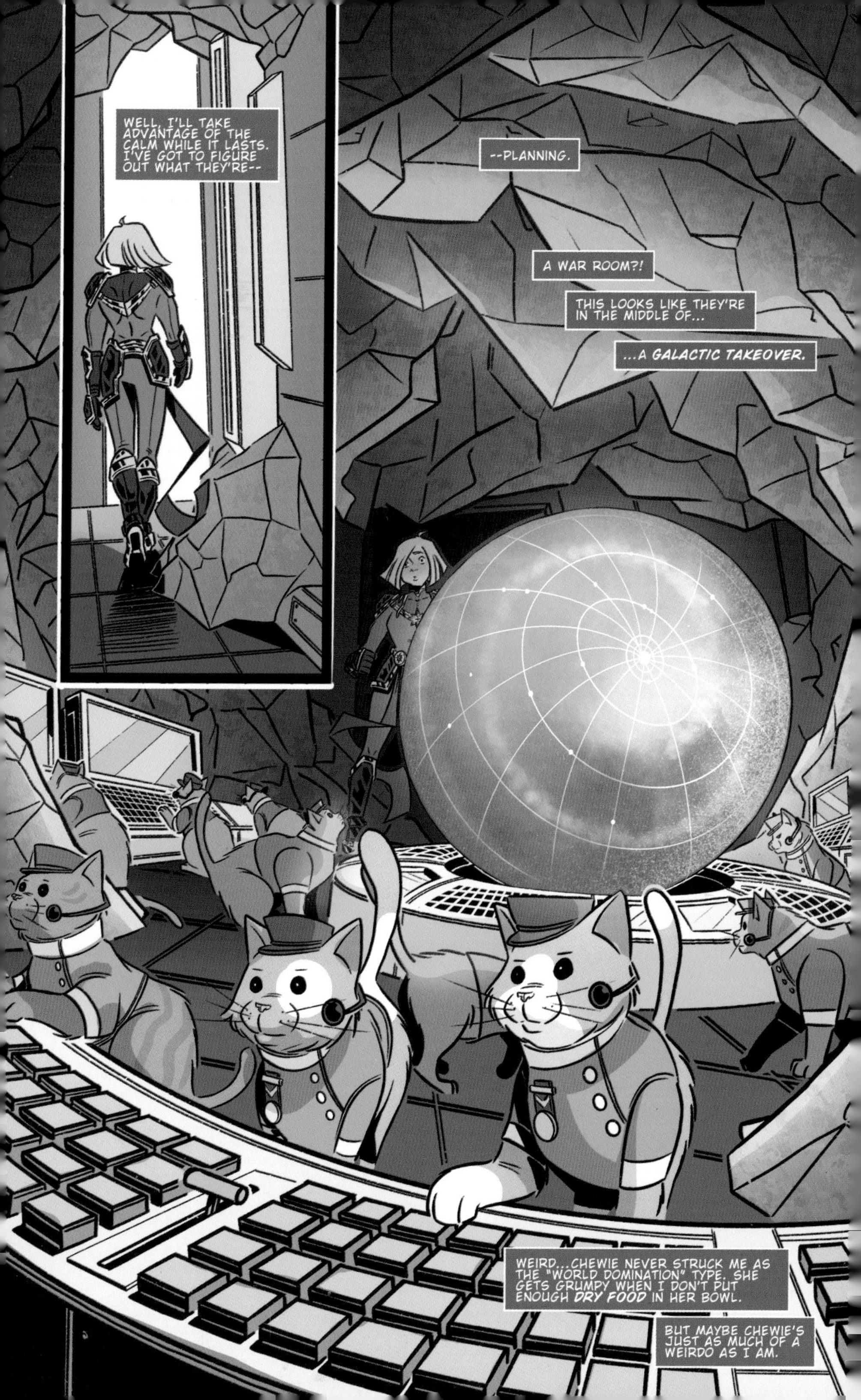
WELL, I'LL TAKE ADVANTAGE OF THE CALM WHILE IT LASTS. I'VE GOT TO FIGURE OUT WHAT THEY'RE--
--PLANNING.
A WAR ROOM?!
THIS LOOKS LIKE THEY'RE IN THE MIDDLE OF...
...A *GALACTIC TAKEOVER.*
WEIRD...CHEWIE NEVER STRUCK ME AS THE "WORLD DOMINATION" TYPE. SHE GETS GRUMPY WHEN I DON'T PUT ENOUGH *DRY FOOD* IN HER BOWL.
BUT MAYBE CHEWIE'S JUST AS MUCH OF A WEIRDO AS I AM.

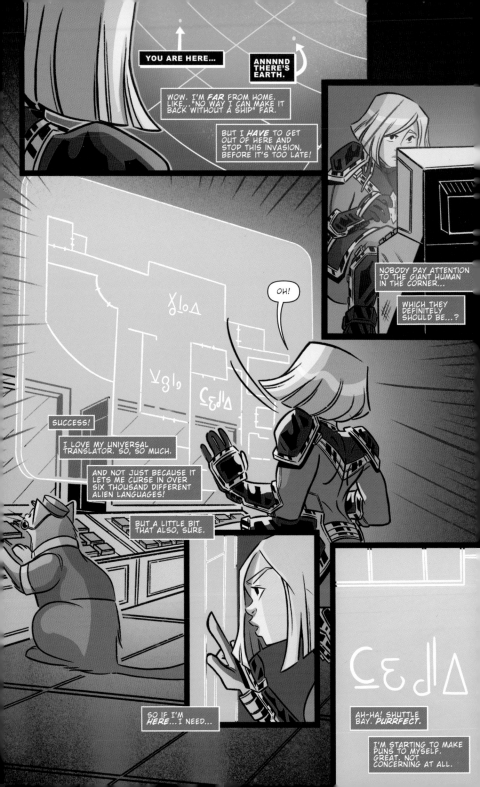

YOU ARE HERE...

ANNNND THERE'S EARTH.

WOW. I'M *FAR* FROM HOME. LIKE... "NO WAY I CAN MAKE IT BACK WITHOUT A SHIP" FAR.

BUT I *HAVE* TO GET OUT OF HERE AND STOP THIS INVASION, BEFORE IT'S TOO LATE!

NOBODY PAY ATTENTION TO THE GIANT HUMAN IN THE CORNER...

WHICH THEY DEFINITELY SHOULD BE...?

OH!

SUCCESS!

I LOVE MY UNIVERSAL TRANSLATOR. SO, SO MUCH.

AND NOT JUST BECAUSE IT LETS ME CURSE IN OVER SIX THOUSAND DIFFERENT ALIEN LANGUAGES!

BUT A LITTLE BIT THAT ALSO, SURE.

SO IF I'M *HERE*...I NEED...

AH-HA! SHUTTLE BAY. *PURRFECT.*

I'M STARTING TO MAKE PUNS TO MYSELF. GREAT. NOT CONCERNING AT ALL.

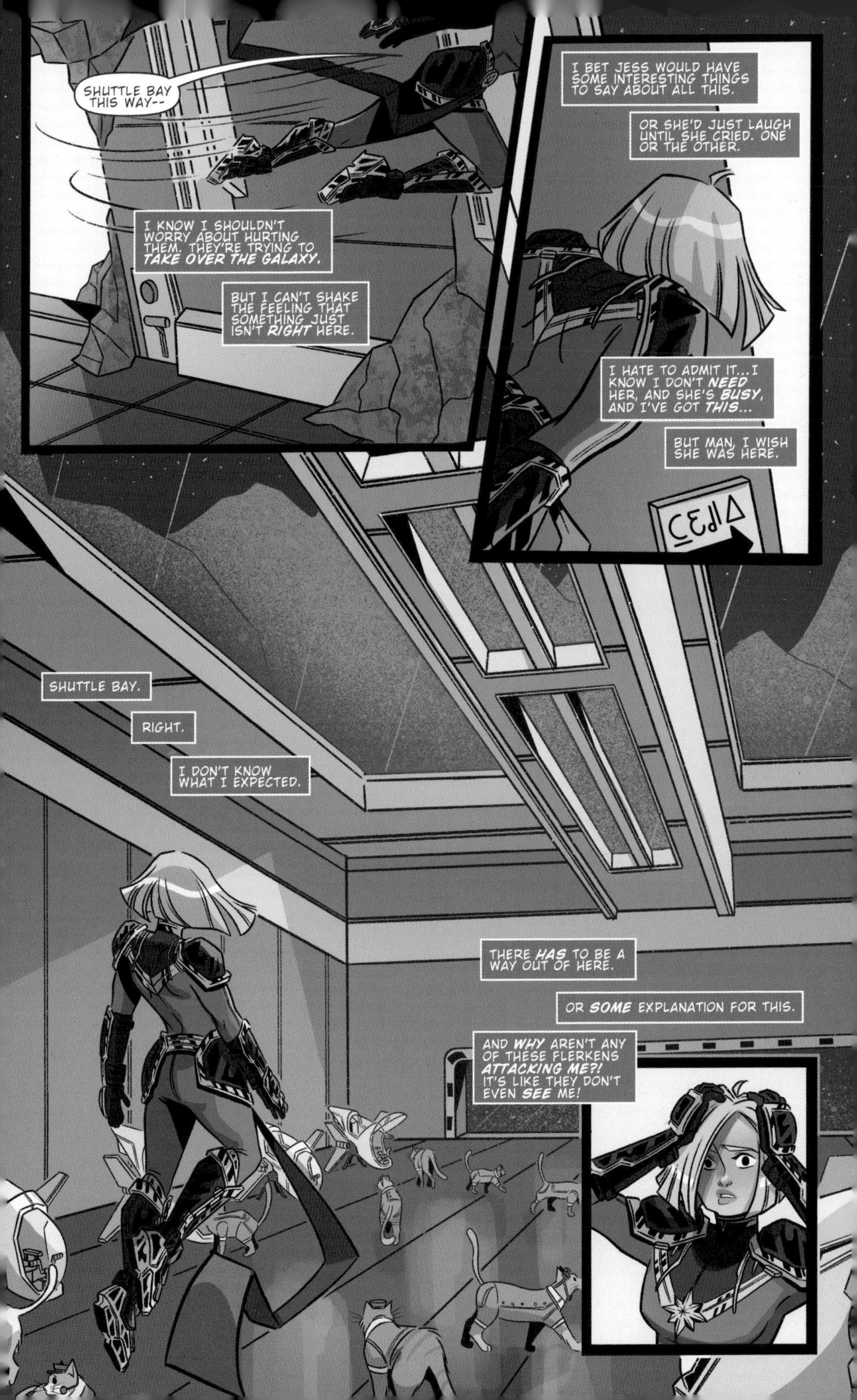
SHUTTLE BAY THIS WAY--
I KNOW I SHOULDN'T WORRY ABOUT HURTING THEM. THEY'RE TRYING TO *TAKE OVER THE GALAXY.*
BUT I CAN'T SHAKE THE FEELING THAT SOMETHING JUST ISN'T *RIGHT* HERE.
I BET JESS WOULD HAVE SOME INTERESTING THINGS TO SAY ABOUT ALL THIS.
OR SHE'D JUST LAUGH UNTIL SHE CRIED. ONE OR THE OTHER.
I HATE TO ADMIT IT...I KNOW I DON'T *NEED* HER, AND SHE'S *BUSY,* AND I'VE GOT *THIS...*
BUT MAN, I WISH SHE WAS HERE.
SHUTTLE BAY.
RIGHT.
I DON'T KNOW WHAT I EXPECTED.
THERE *HAS* TO BE A WAY OUT OF HERE.
OR *SOME* EXPLANATION FOR THIS.
AND *WHY* AREN'T ANY OF THESE FLERKENS *ATTACKING ME?!* IT'S LIKE THEY DON'T EVEN *SEE* ME!

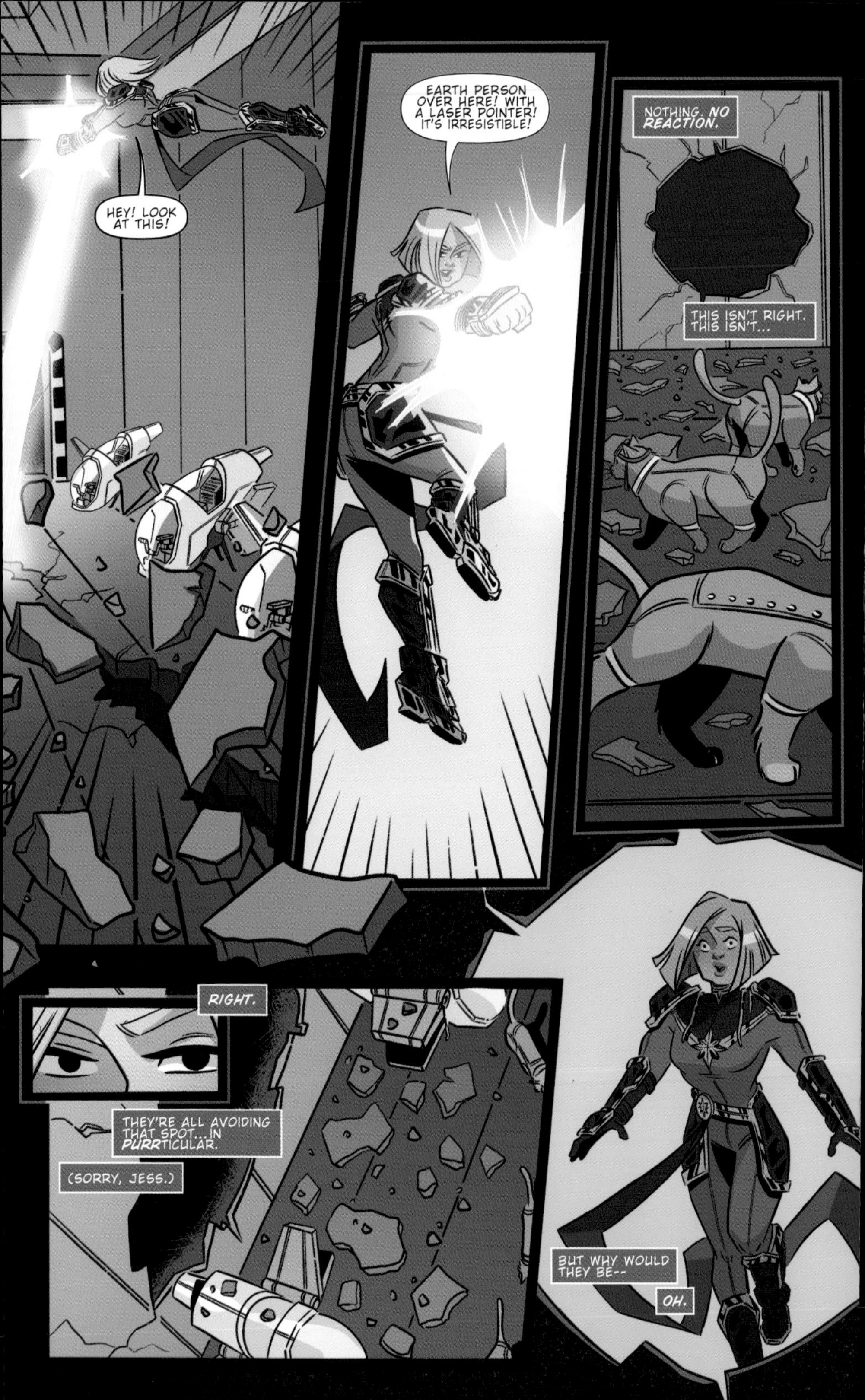
HEY! LOOK AT THIS!
EARTH PERSON OVER HERE! WITH A LASER POINTER! IT'S IRRESISTIBLE!
NOTHING. NO REACTION.
THIS ISN'T RIGHT. THIS ISN'T...
RIGHT.
THEY'RE ALL AVOIDING THAT SPOT... IN PURRTICULAR.
(SORRY, JESS.)
BUT WHY WOULD THEY BE--
OH.

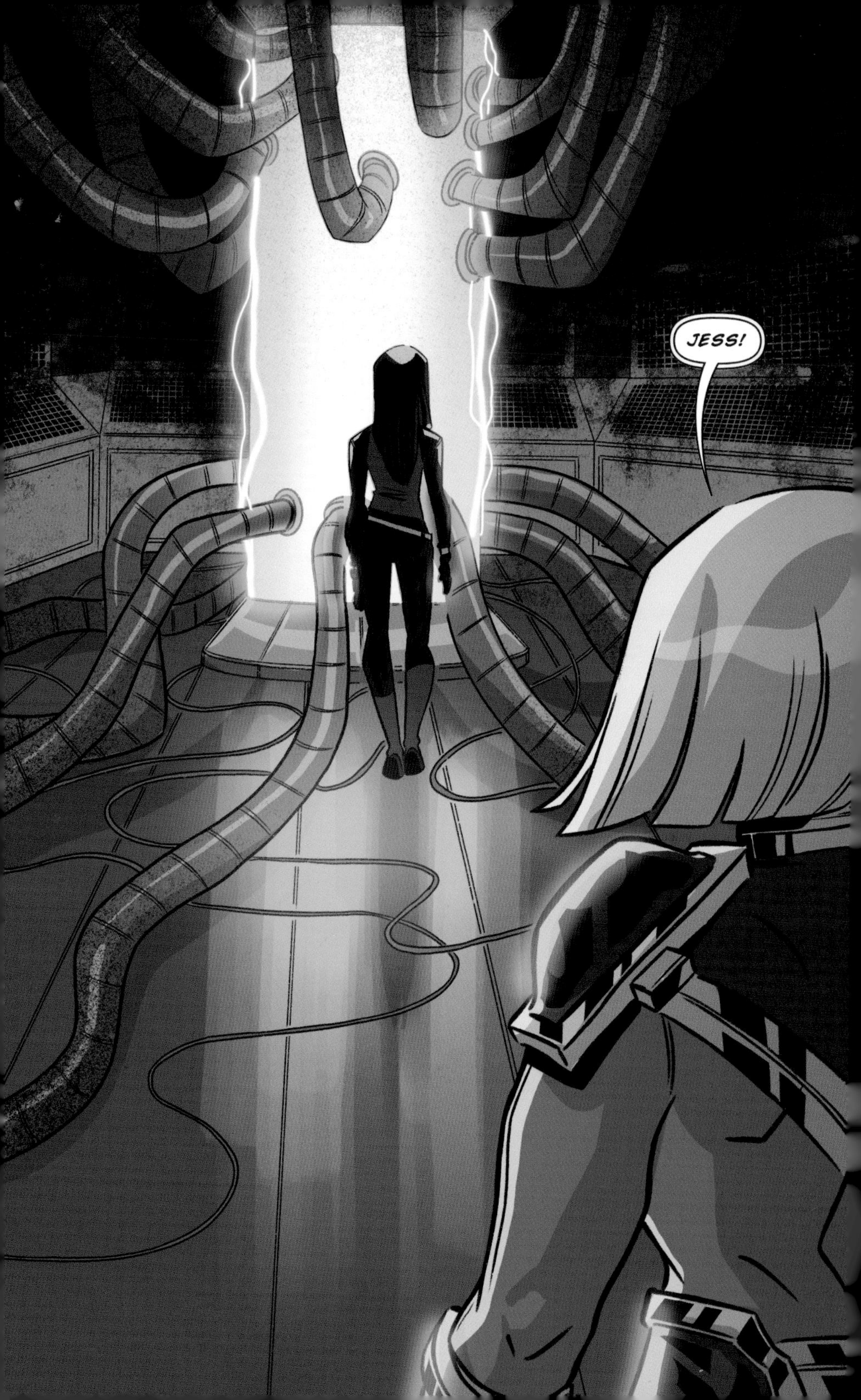
JESS!

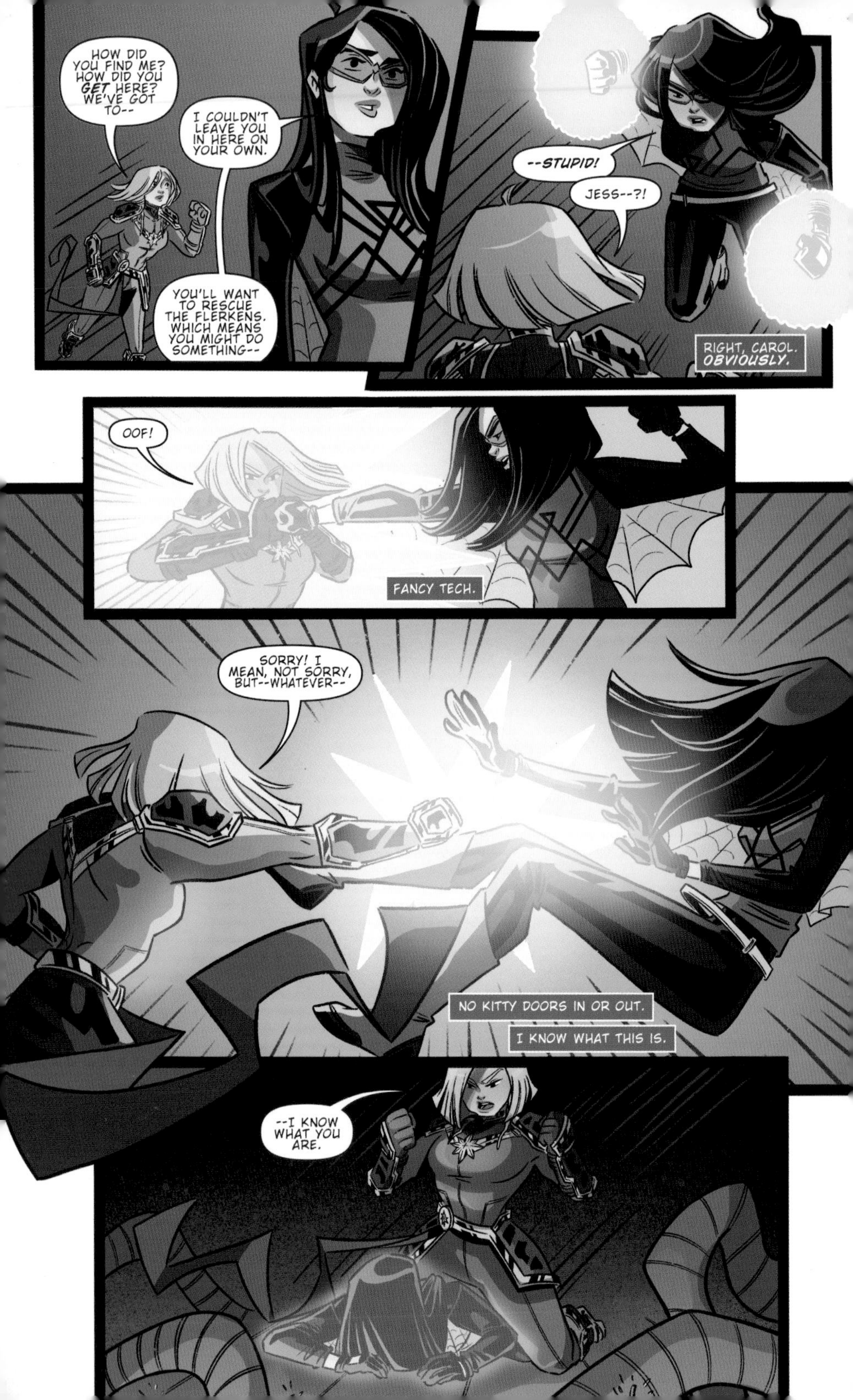
HOW DID YOU FIND ME? HOW DID YOU GET HERE? WE'VE GOT TO--
I COULDN'T LEAVE YOU IN HERE ON YOUR OWN.
YOU'LL WANT TO RESCUE THE FLERKENS. WHICH MEANS YOU MIGHT DO SOMETHING--
--STUPID!
JESS--?!
RIGHT, CAROL. OBVIOUSLY.
OOF!
FANCY TECH.
SORRY! I MEAN, NOT SORRY, BUT--WHATEVER--
NO KITTY DOORS IN OR OUT.
I KNOW WHAT THIS IS.
--I KNOW WHAT YOU ARE.

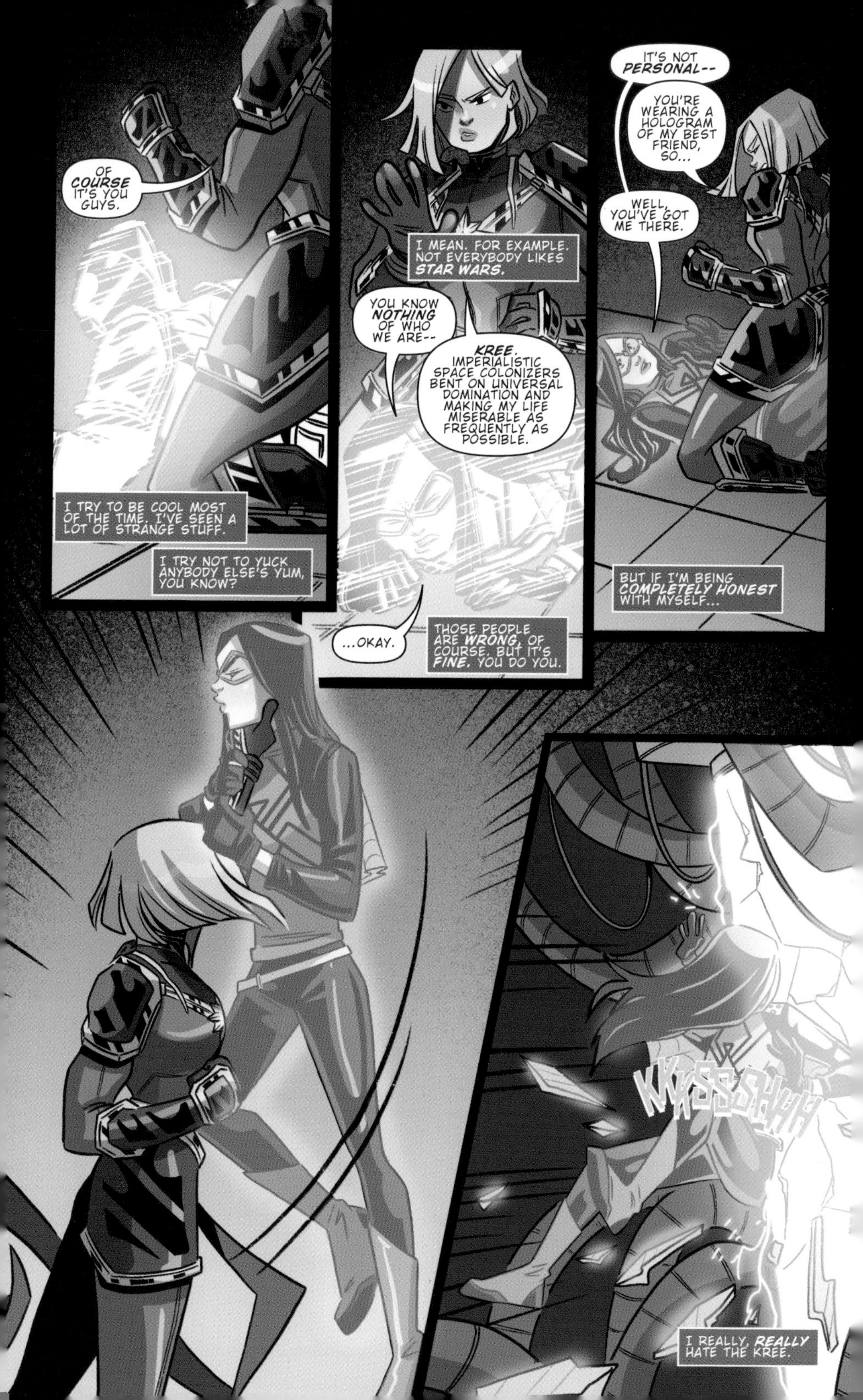

OF COURSE IT'S YOU GUYS.
I TRY TO BE COOL MOST OF THE TIME. I'VE SEEN A LOT OF STRANGE STUFF.
I TRY NOT TO YUCK ANYBODY ELSE'S YUM, YOU KNOW?
I MEAN. FOR EXAMPLE. NOT EVERYBODY LIKES STAR WARS.
YOU KNOW NOTHING OF WHO WE ARE--
KREE. IMPERIALISTIC SPACE COLONIZERS BENT ON UNIVERSAL DOMINATION AND MAKING MY LIFE MISERABLE AS FREQUENTLY AS POSSIBLE.
...OKAY.
THOSE PEOPLE ARE WRONG, OF COURSE. BUT IT'S FINE. YOU DO YOU.
IT'S NOT PERSONAL--
YOU'RE WEARING A HOLOGRAM OF MY BEST FRIEND, SO...
WELL, YOU'VE GOT ME THERE.
BUT IF I'M BEING COMPLETELY HONEST WITH MYSELF...
KKKSSSHHH
I REALLY, REALLY HATE THE KREE.

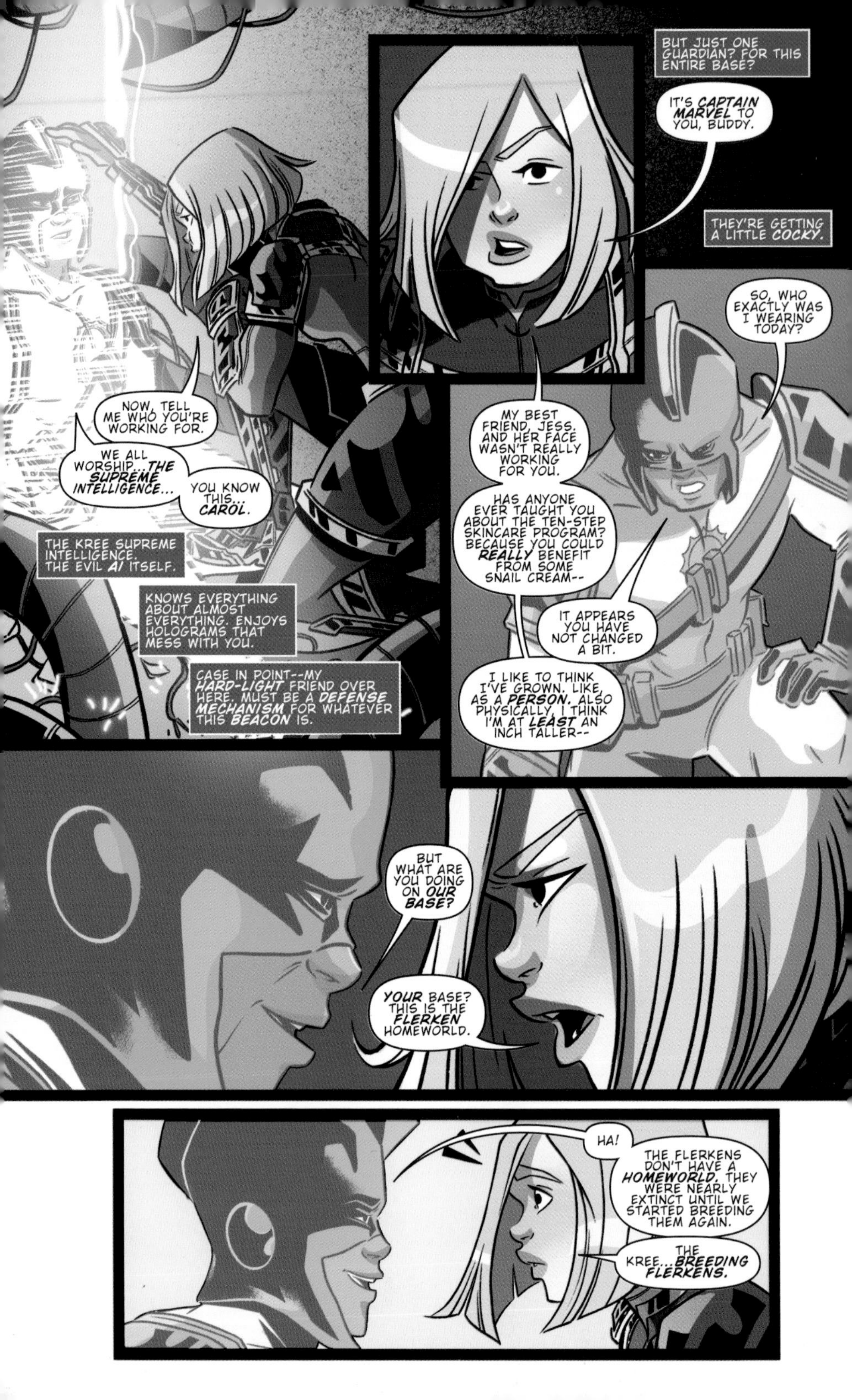
BUT JUST ONE GUARDIAN? FOR THIS ENTIRE BASE?
IT'S CAPTAIN MARVEL TO YOU, BUDDY.
THEY'RE GETTING A LITTLE COCKY.
NOW, TELL ME WHO YOU'RE WORKING FOR.
WE ALL WORSHIP... THE SUPREME INTELLIGENCE...
YOU KNOW THIS... CAROL.
THE KREE SUPREME INTELLIGENCE. THE EVIL AI ITSELF.
KNOWS EVERYTHING ABOUT ALMOST EVERYTHING. ENJOYS HOLOGRAMS THAT MESS WITH YOU.
CASE IN POINT--MY HARD-LIGHT FRIEND OVER HERE. MUST BE A DEFENSE MECHANISM FOR WHATEVER THIS BEACON IS.
SO, WHO EXACTLY WAS I WEARING TODAY?
MY BEST FRIEND, JESS. AND HER FACE WASN'T REALLY WORKING FOR YOU.
HAS ANYONE EVER TAUGHT YOU ABOUT THE TEN-STEP SKINCARE PROGRAM? BECAUSE YOU COULD REALLY BENEFIT FROM SOME SNAIL CREAM--
IT APPEARS YOU HAVE NOT CHANGED A BIT.
I LIKE TO THINK I'VE GROWN. LIKE, AS A PERSON. ALSO PHYSICALLY, I THINK I'M AT LEAST AN INCH TALLER--
BUT WHAT ARE YOU DOING ON OUR BASE?
YOUR BASE? THIS IS THE FLERKEN HOMEWORLD.
HA!
THE FLERKENS DON'T HAVE A HOMEWORLD. THEY WERE NEARLY EXTINCT UNTIL WE STARTED BREEDING THEM AGAIN.
THE KREE... BREEDING FLERKENS.

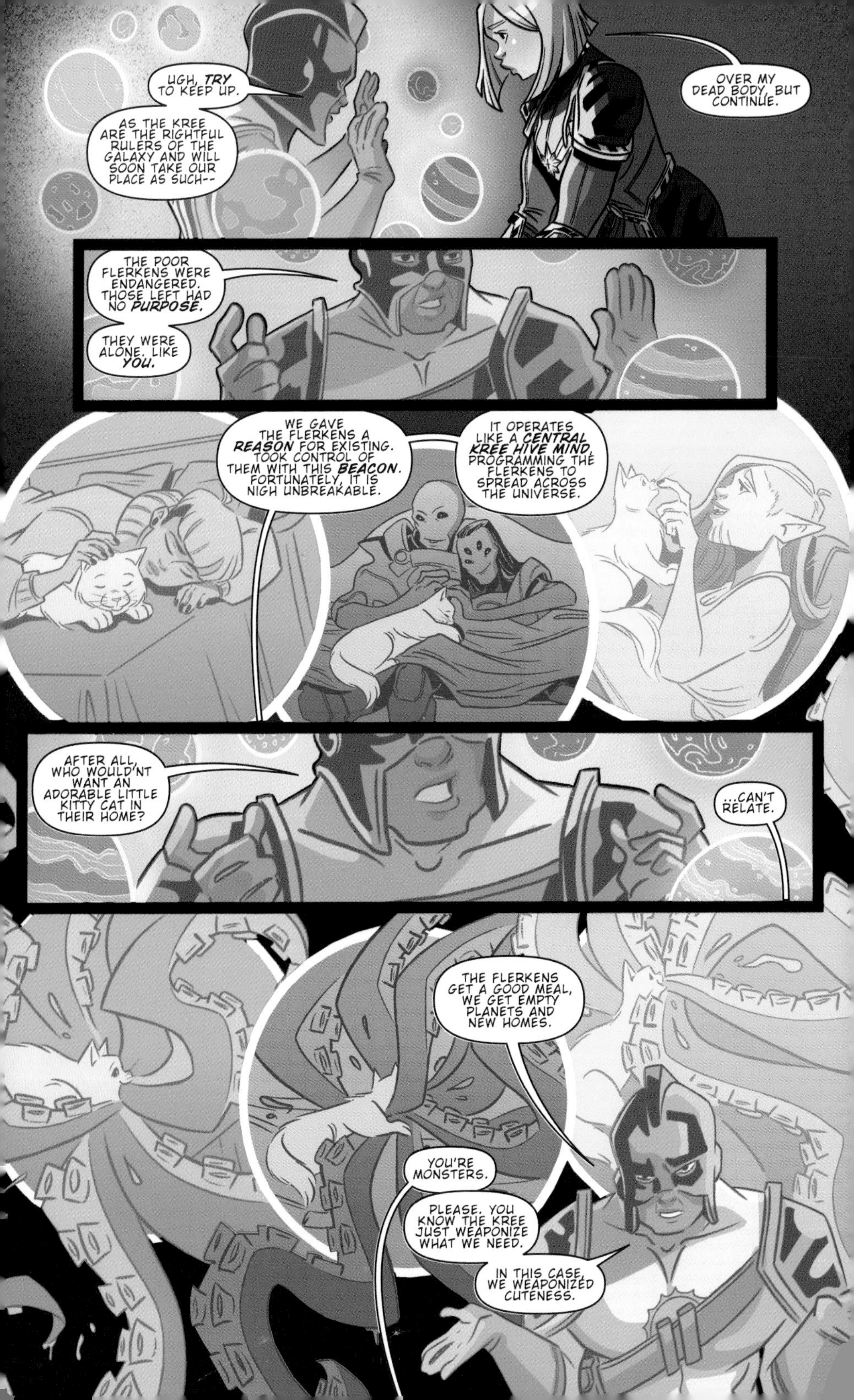
UGH, TRY TO KEEP UP.
AS THE KREE ARE THE RIGHTFUL RULERS OF THE GALAXY AND WILL SOON TAKE OUR PLACE AS SUCH--
OVER MY DEAD BODY, BUT CONTINUE.
THE POOR FLERKENS WERE ENDANGERED. THOSE LEFT HAD NO PURPOSE.
THEY WERE ALONE. LIKE YOU.
WE GAVE THE FLERKENS A REASON FOR EXISTING. TOOK CONTROL OF THEM WITH THIS BEACON. FORTUNATELY, IT IS NIGH UNBREAKABLE.
IT OPERATES LIKE A CENTRAL KREE HIVE MIND, PROGRAMMING THE FLERKENS TO SPREAD ACROSS THE UNIVERSE.
AFTER ALL, WHO WOULD'NT WANT AN ADORABLE LITTLE KITTY CAT IN THEIR HOME?
...CAN'T RELATE.
THE FLERKENS GET A GOOD MEAL, WE GET EMPTY PLANETS AND NEW HOMES.
YOU'RE MONSTERS.
PLEASE. YOU KNOW THE KREE JUST WEAPONIZE WHAT WE NEED.
IN THIS CASE, WE WEAPONIZED CUTENESS.

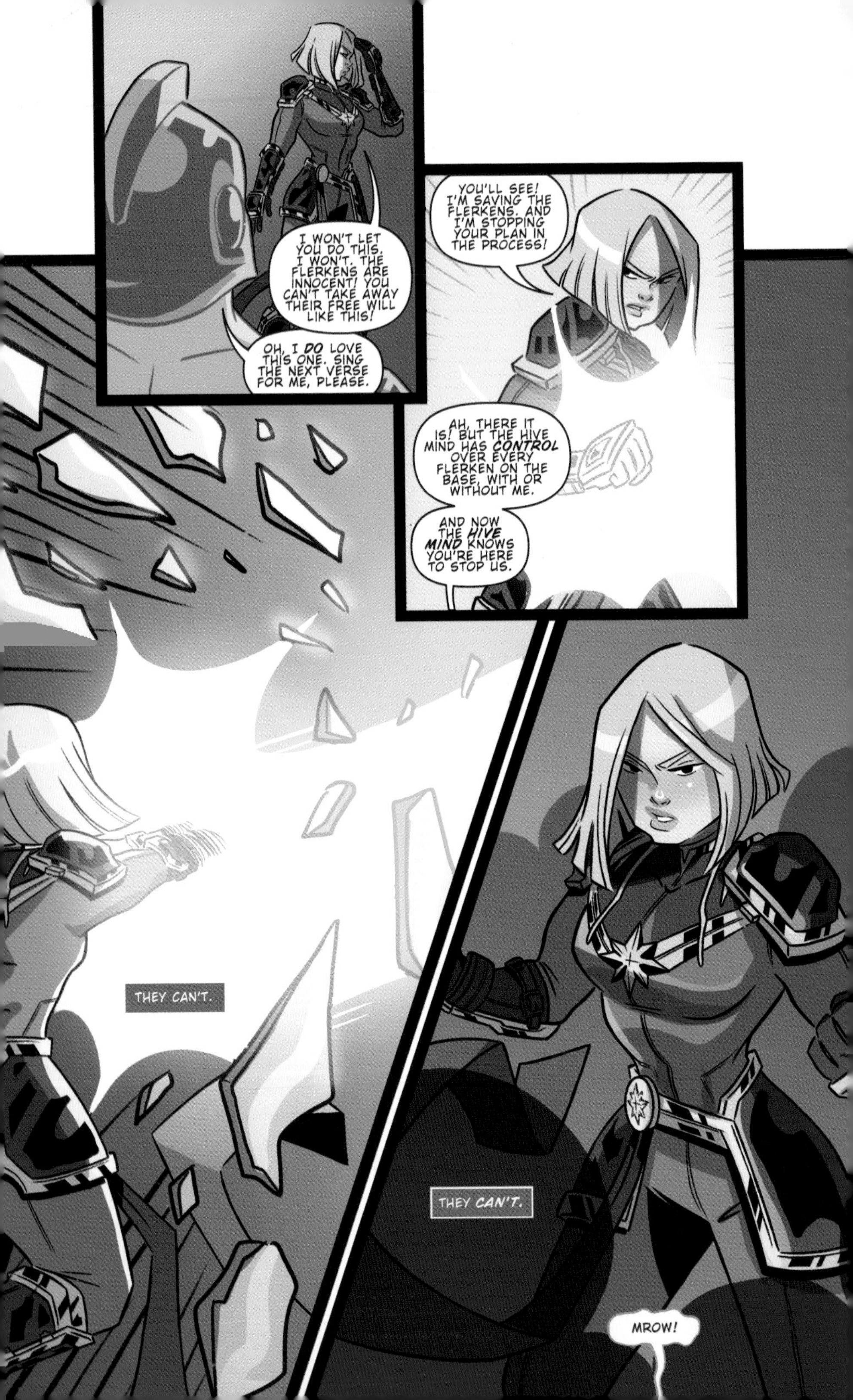
I WON'T LET YOU DO THIS. I WON'T. THE FLERKENS ARE INNOCENT! YOU CAN'T TAKE AWAY THEIR FREE WILL LIKE THIS!
OH, I DO LOVE THIS ONE. SING THE NEXT VERSE FOR ME, PLEASE.
YOU'LL SEE! I'M SAVING THE FLERKENS. AND I'M STOPPING YOUR PLAN IN THE PROCESS!
AH, THERE IT IS! BUT THE HIVE MIND HAS CONTROL OVER EVERY FLERKEN ON THE BASE, WITH OR WITHOUT ME.
AND NOW THE HIVE MIND KNOWS YOU'RE HERE TO STOP US.
THEY CAN'T.
THEY CAN'T.
MROW!

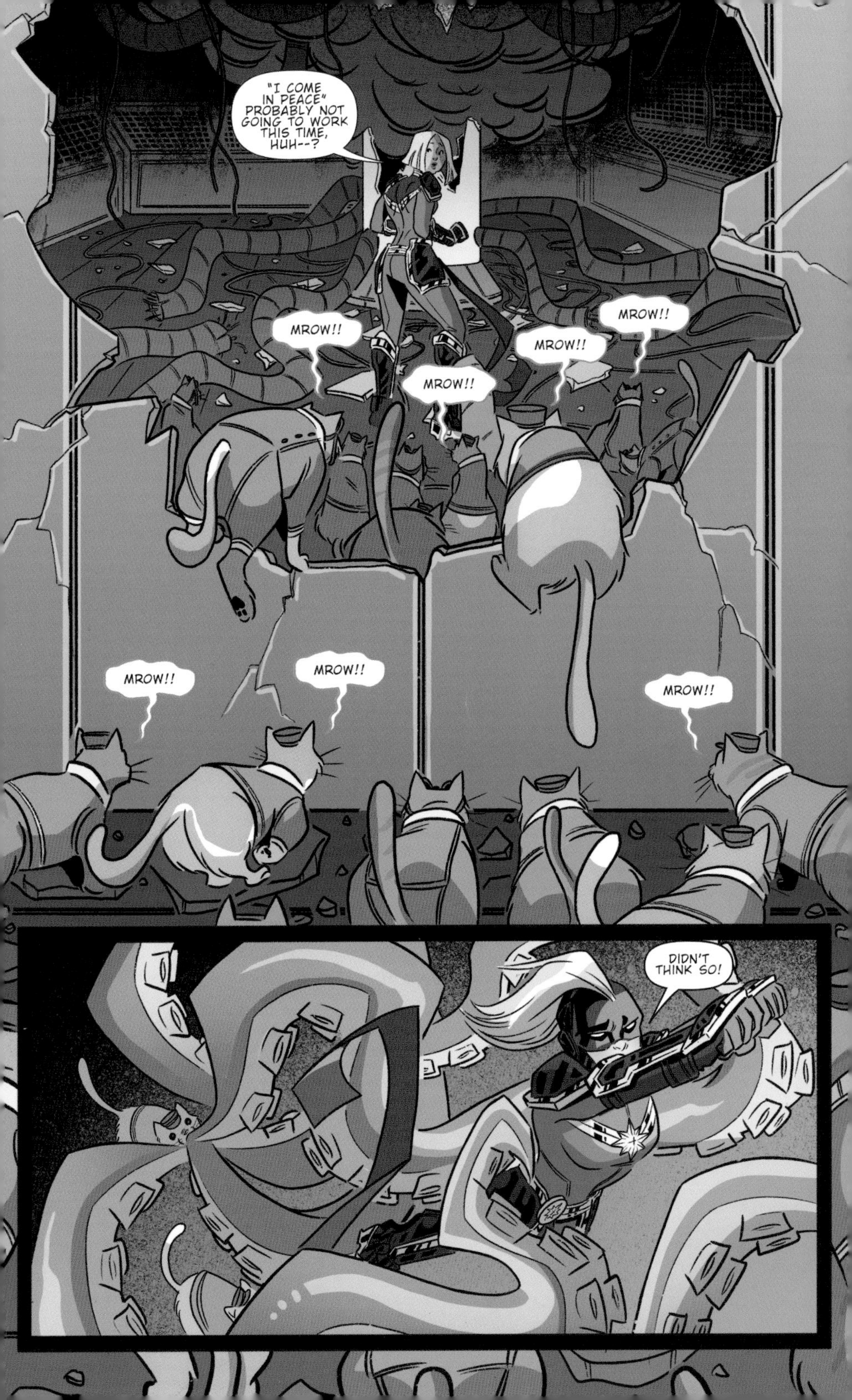
"I COME IN PEACE" PROBABLY NOT GOING TO WORK THIS TIME, HUH--?
MROW!!
MROW!!
MROW!!
MROW!!
MROW!!
MROW!!
MROW!!
DIDN'T THINK SO!

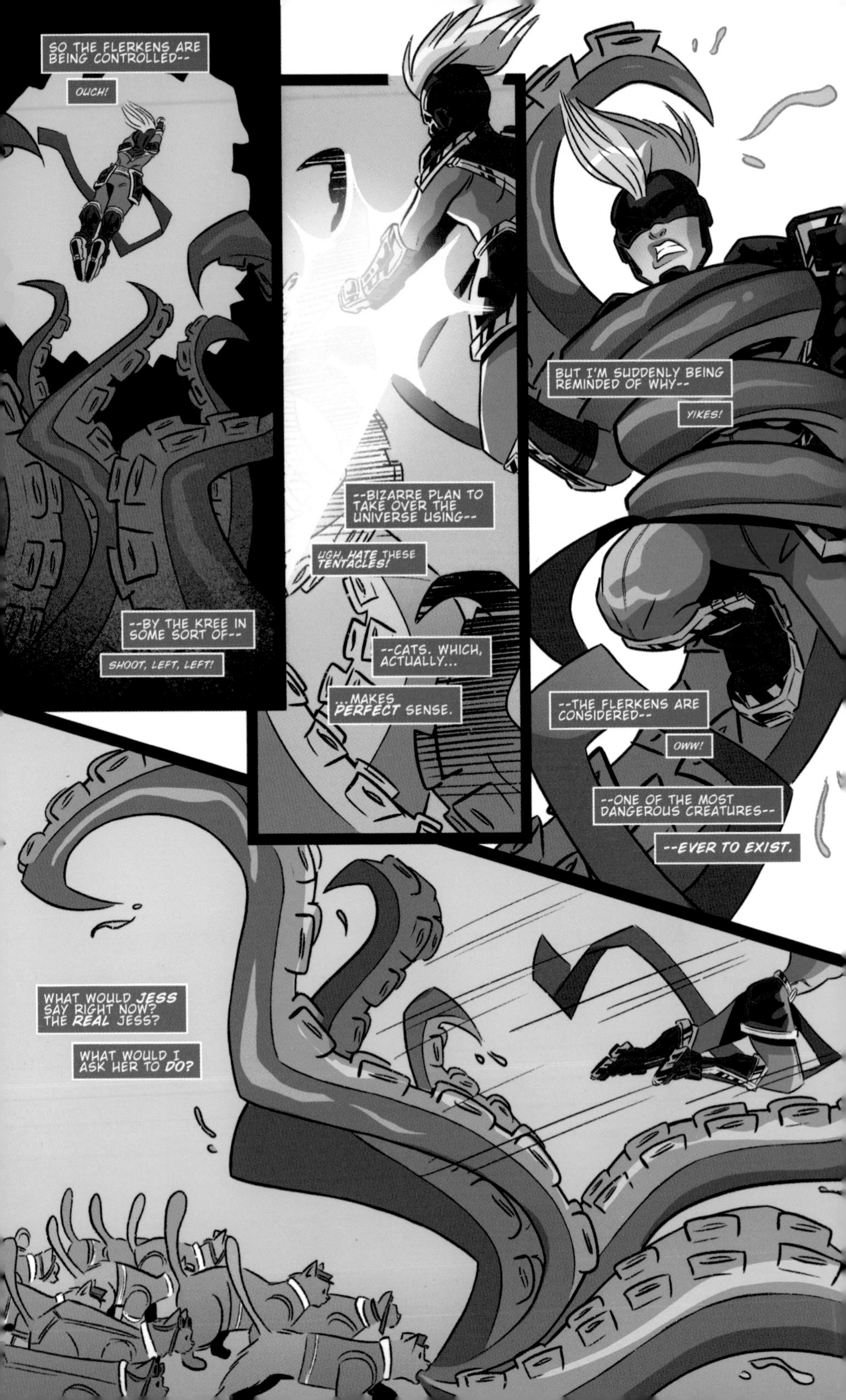
SO THE FLERKENS ARE BEING CONTROLLED--
OUCH!
--BY THE KREE IN SOME SORT OF--
SHOOT, LEFT, LEFT!
--BIZARRE PLAN TO TAKE OVER THE UNIVERSE USING--
UGH, HATE THESE TENTACLES!
--CATS. WHICH, ACTUALLY...
...MAKES PERFECT SENSE.
BUT I'M SUDDENLY BEING REMINDED OF WHY--
YIKES!
--THE FLERKENS ARE CONSIDERED--
OWW!
--ONE OF THE MOST DANGEROUS CREATURES--
--EVER TO EXIST.
WHAT WOULD JESS SAY RIGHT NOW? THE REAL JESS?
WHAT WOULD I ASK HER TO DO?

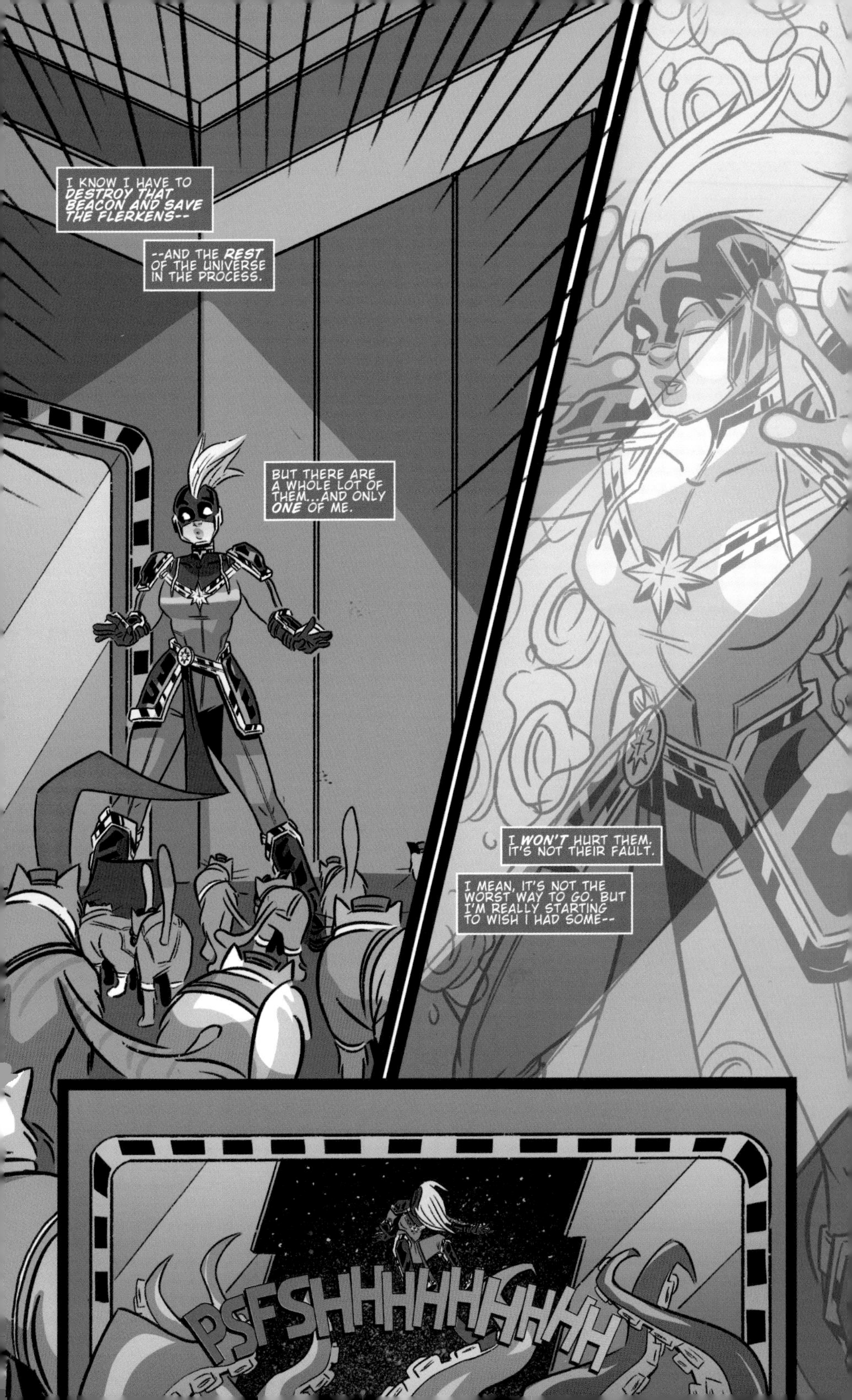
I KNOW I HAVE TO DESTROY THAT BEACON AND SAVE THE FLERKENS--
--AND THE REST OF THE UNIVERSE IN THE PROCESS.
BUT THERE ARE A WHOLE LOT OF THEM...AND ONLY ONE OF ME.
I WON'T HURT THEM. IT'S NOT THEIR FAULT.
I MEAN, IT'S NOT THE WORST WAY TO GO. BUT I'M REALLY STARTING TO WISH I HAD SOME--
PSFSHHHHHHHHHH

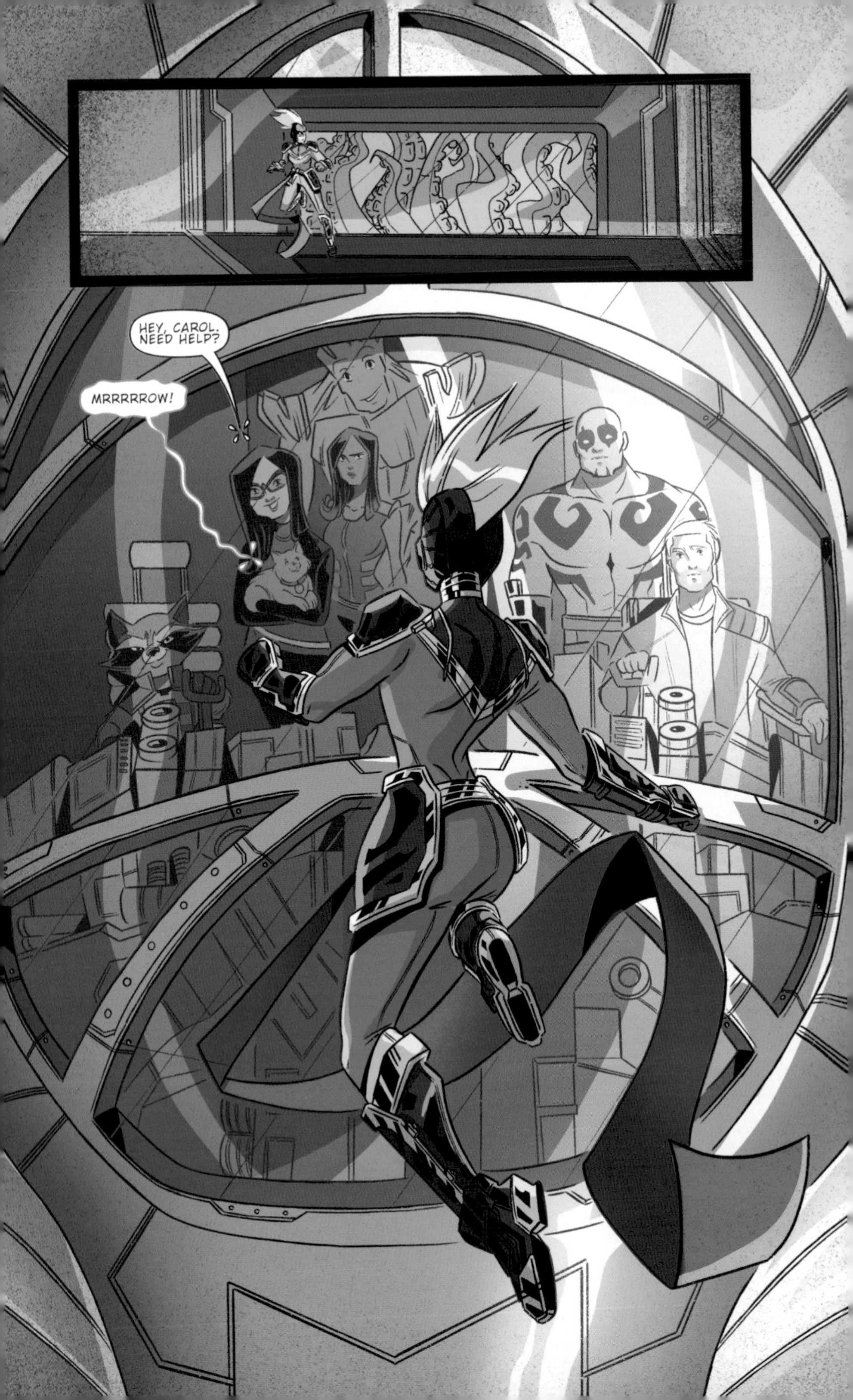
HEY, CAROL. NEED HELP?
MRRRRROW!

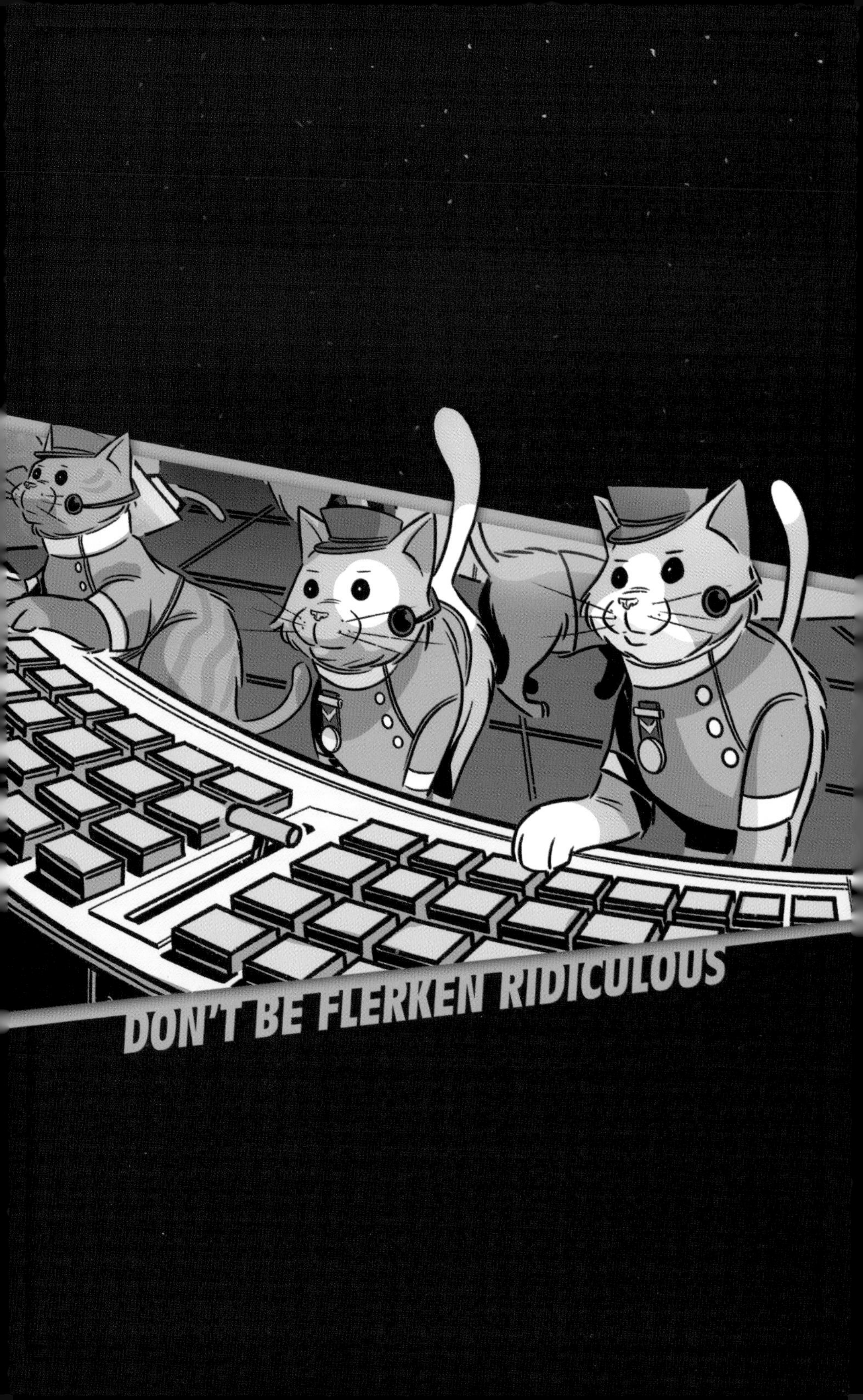
DON'T BE FLERKEN RIDICULOUS

ART BY: SWEENEY BOO

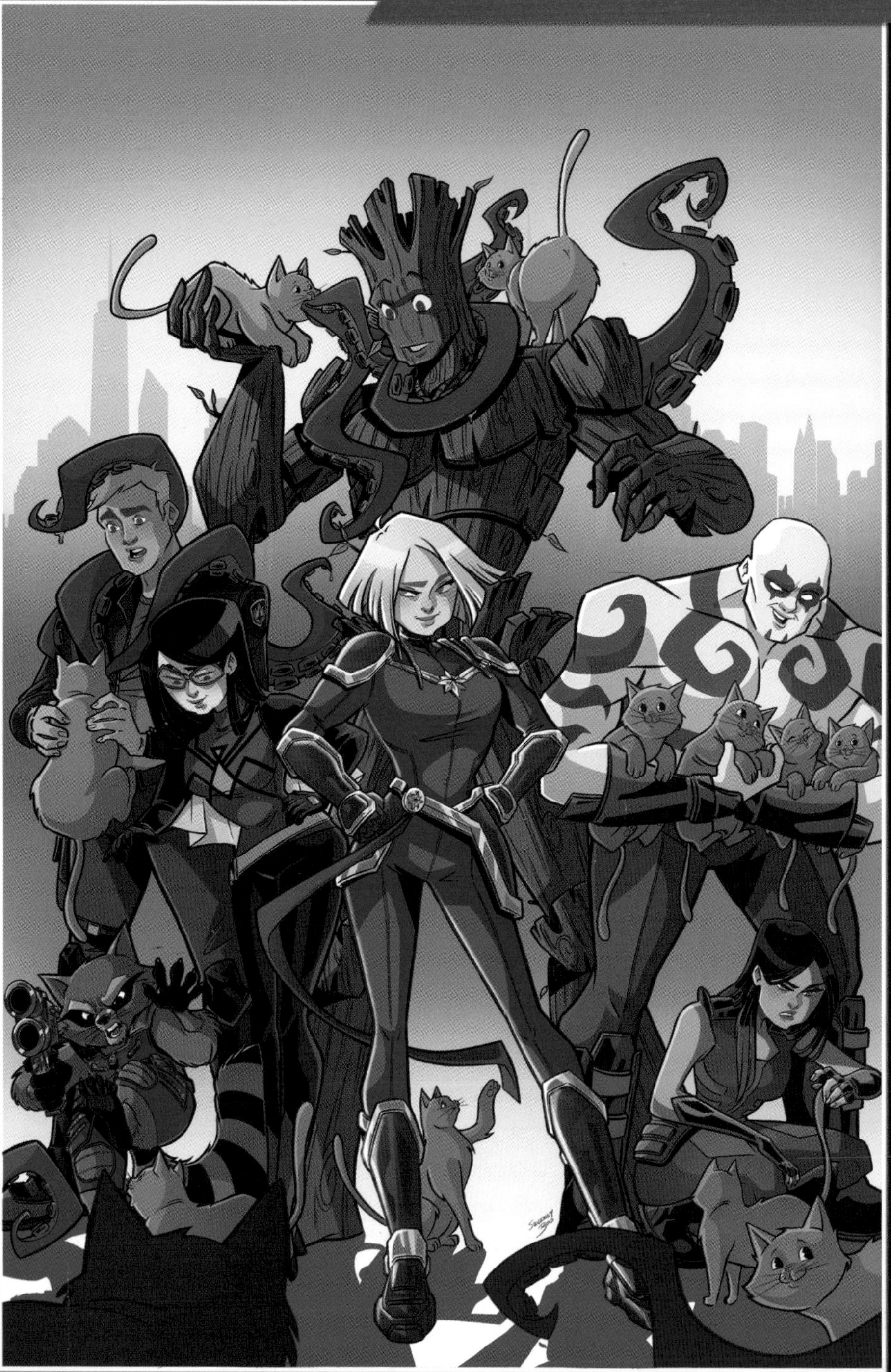

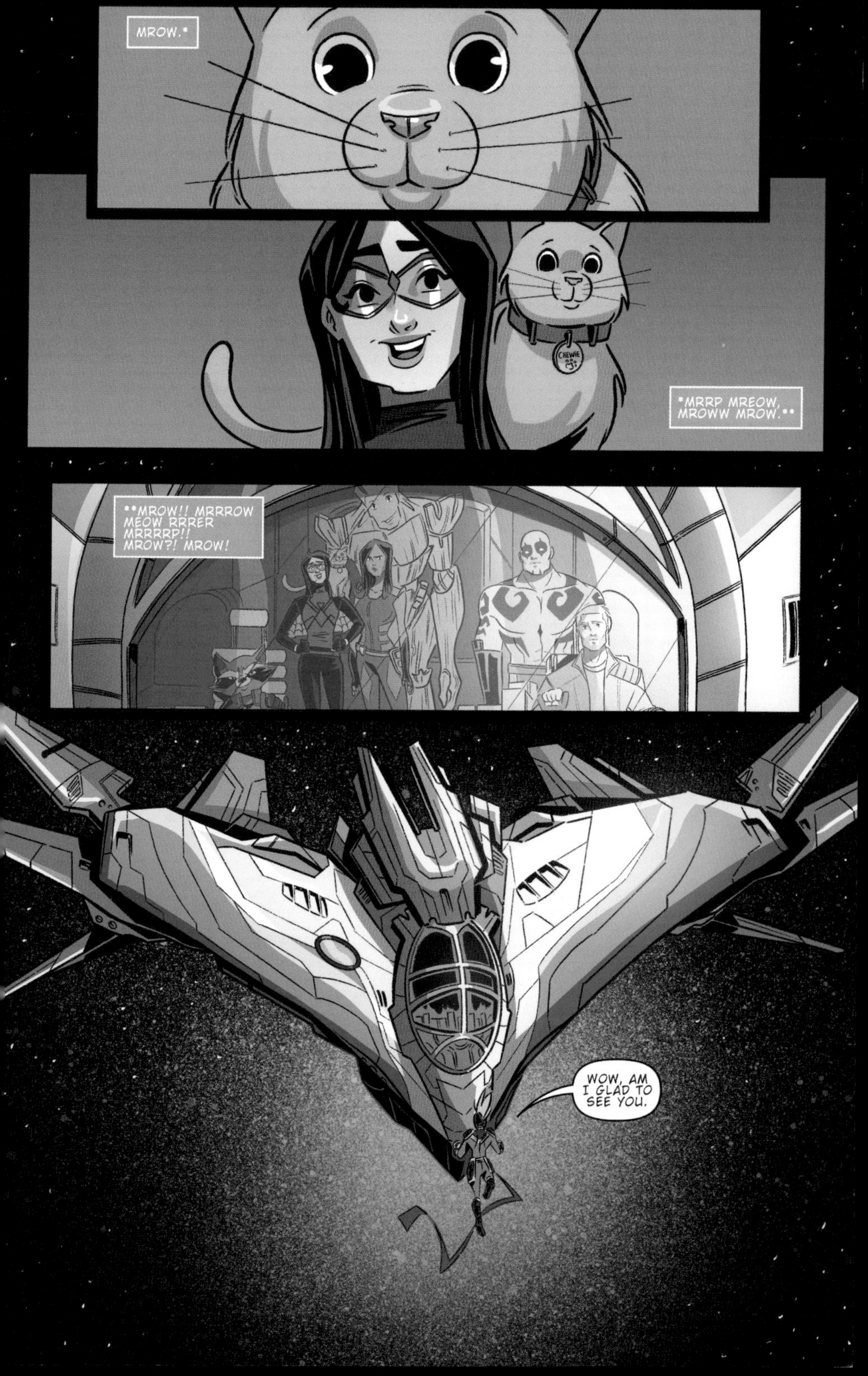
MROW.*
*MRRP MREOW, MROWW MROW.**
**MROW!! MRRROW MEOW RRRER MRRRRP!! MROW?! MROW!
CHEWIE
WOW, AM I GLAD TO SEE YOU.

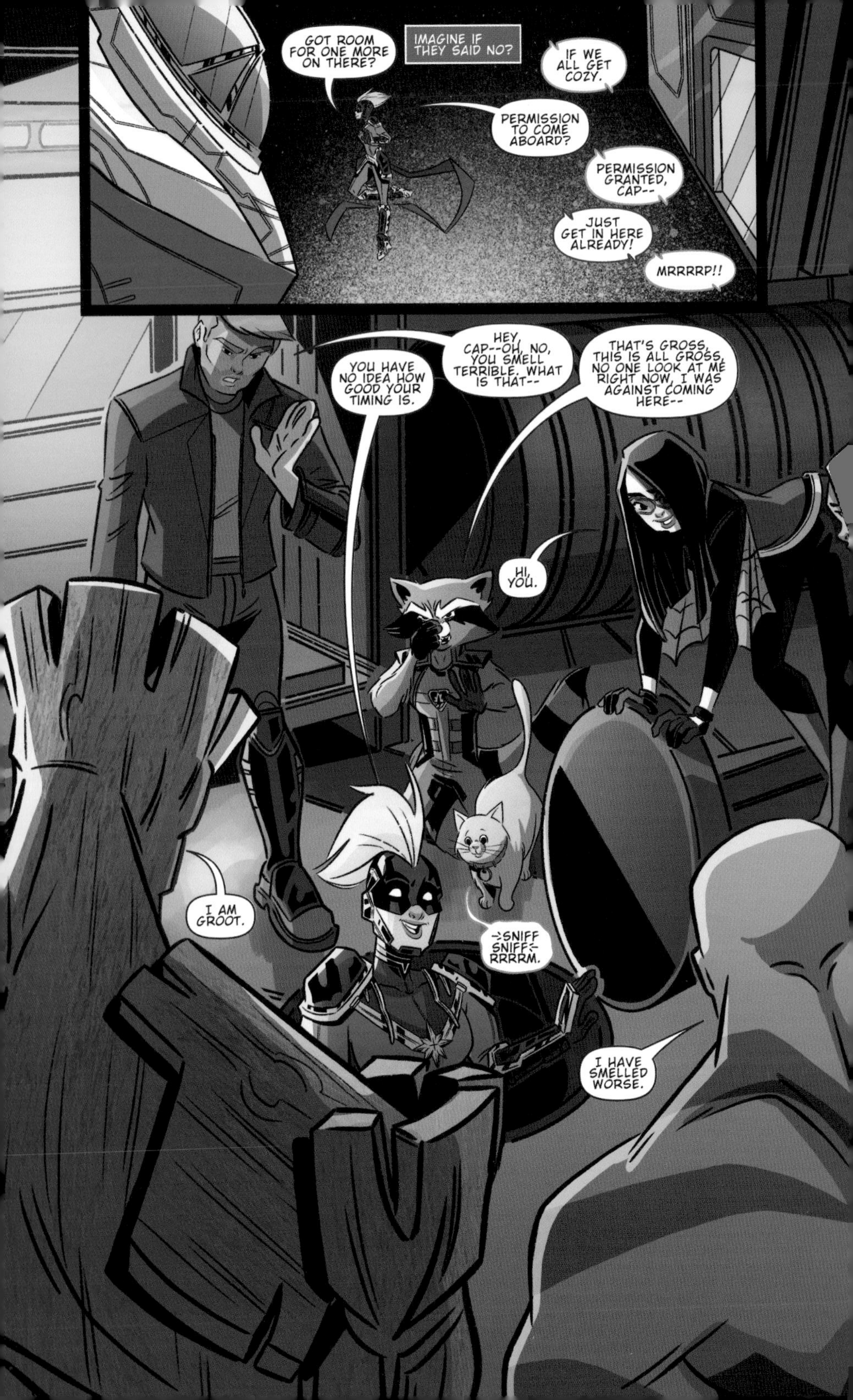
GOT ROOM FOR ONE MORE ON THERE?
IMAGINE IF THEY SAID NO?
IF WE ALL GET COZY.
PERMISSION TO COME ABOARD?
PERMISSION GRANTED, CAP--
JUST GET IN HERE ALREADY!
MRRRRP!!
YOU HAVE NO IDEA HOW GOOD YOUR TIMING IS.
HEY, CAP--OH, NO, YOU SMELL TERRIBLE. WHAT IS THAT--
THAT'S GROSS, THIS IS ALL GROSS, NO ONE LOOK AT ME RIGHT NOW, I WAS AGAINST COMING HERE--
HI, YOU.
I AM GROOT.
SNIFF SNIFF RRRRM.
I HAVE SMELLED WORSE.

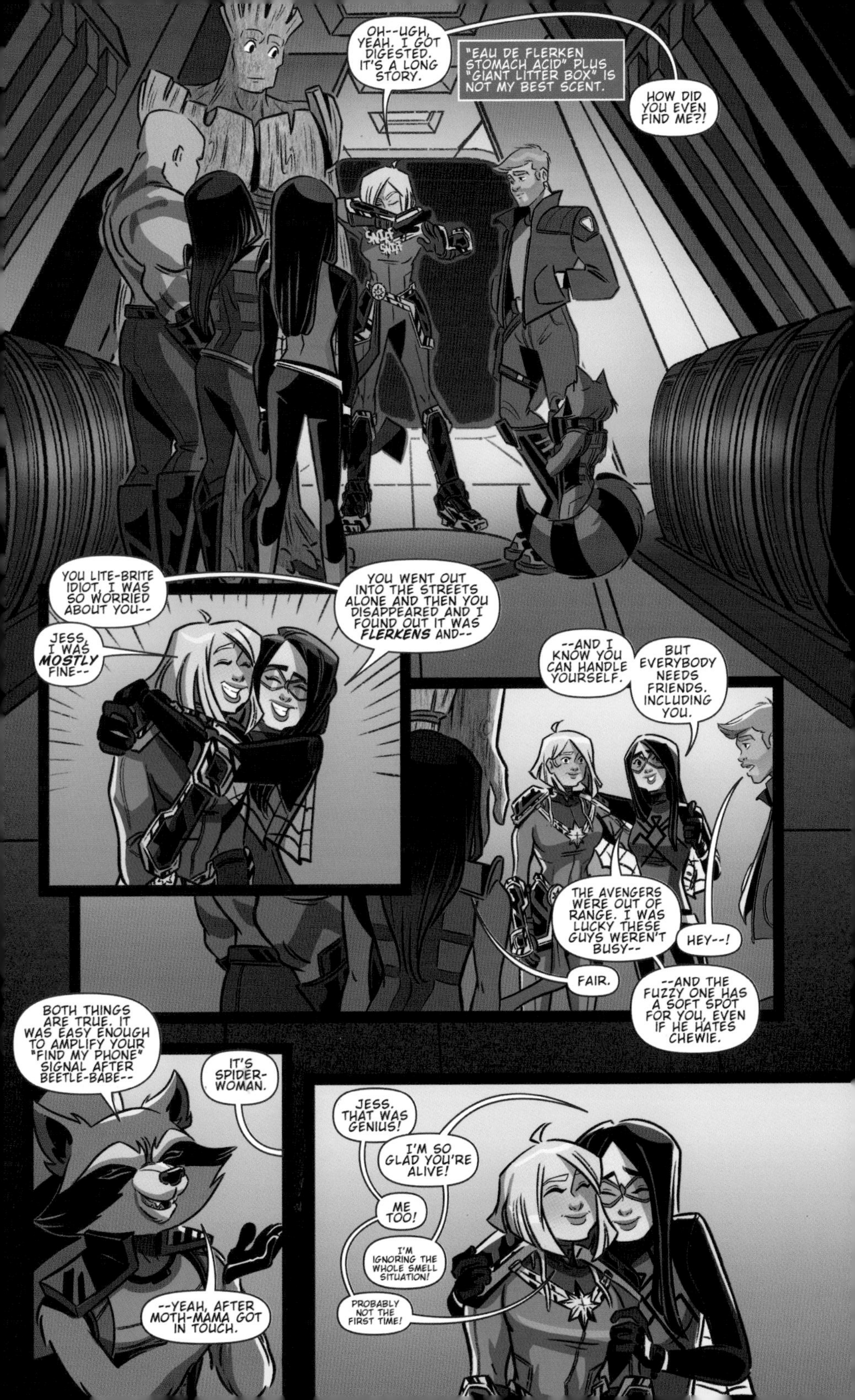
OH--UGH, YEAH. I GOT DIGESTED. IT'S A LONG STORY.
"EAU DE FLERKEN STOMACH ACID" PLUS "GIANT LITTER BOX" IS NOT MY BEST SCENT.
HOW DID YOU EVEN FIND ME?!
SNIFF SNIFF
YOU LITE-BRITE IDIOT, I WAS SO WORRIED ABOUT YOU--
YOU WENT OUT INTO THE STREETS ALONE AND THEN YOU DISAPPEARED AND I FOUND OUT IT WAS *FLERKENS* AND--
JESS, I WAS *MOSTLY* FINE--
--AND I KNOW YOU CAN HANDLE YOURSELF.
BUT EVERYBODY NEEDS FRIENDS. INCLUDING YOU.
THE AVENGERS WERE OUT OF RANGE. I WAS LUCKY THESE GUYS WEREN'T BUSY--
HEY--!
FAIR.
--AND THE FUZZY ONE HAS A SOFT SPOT FOR YOU, EVEN IF HE HATES CHEWIE.
BOTH THINGS ARE TRUE. IT WAS EASY ENOUGH TO AMPLIFY YOUR "FIND MY PHONE" SIGNAL AFTER BEETLE-BABE--
IT'S SPIDER-WOMAN.
--YEAH, AFTER MOTH-MAMA GOT IN TOUCH.
JESS. THAT WAS GENIUS!
I'M SO GLAD YOU'RE ALIVE!
ME TOO!
I'M IGNORING THE WHOLE SMELL SITUATION!
PROBABLY NOT THE FIRST TIME!

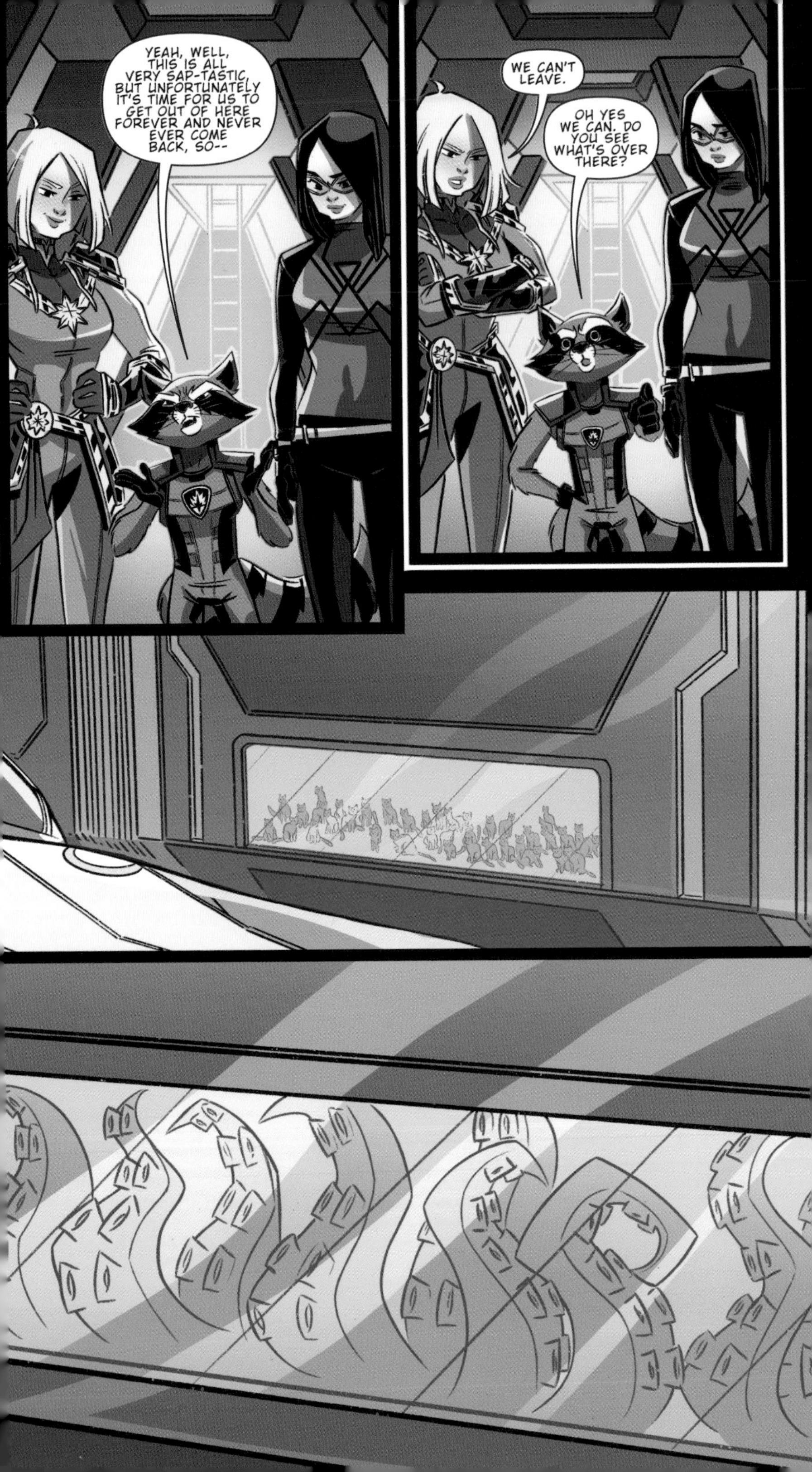
YEAH, WELL, THIS IS ALL VERY SAP-TASTIC, BUT UNFORTUNATELY IT'S TIME FOR US TO GET OUT OF HERE FOREVER AND NEVER EVER COME BACK, SO--
WE CAN'T LEAVE.
OH YES WE CAN. DO YOU SEE WHAT'S OVER THERE?

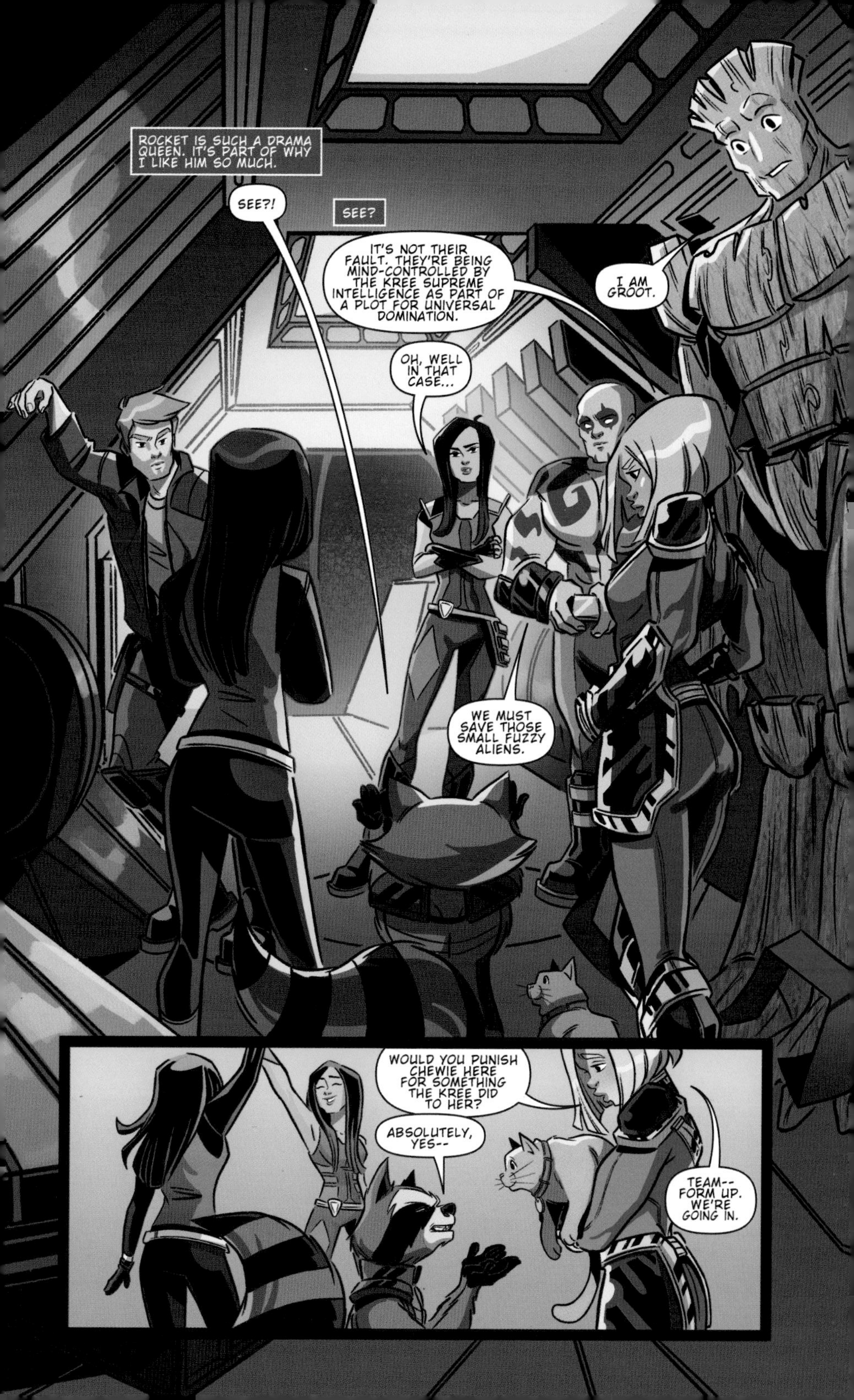
ROCKET IS SUCH A DRAMA QUEEN. IT'S PART OF WHY I LIKE HIM SO MUCH.
SEE?!
SEE?
IT'S NOT THEIR FAULT. THEY'RE BEING MIND-CONTROLLED BY THE KREE SUPREME INTELLIGENCE AS PART OF A PLOT FOR UNIVERSAL DOMINATION.
I AM GROOT.
OH, WELL IN THAT CASE...
WE MUST SAVE THOSE SMALL FUZZY ALIENS.
WOULD YOU PUNISH CHEWIE HERE FOR SOMETHING THE KREE DID TO HER?
ABSOLUTELY, YES--
TEAM-- FORM UP. WE'RE GOING IN.

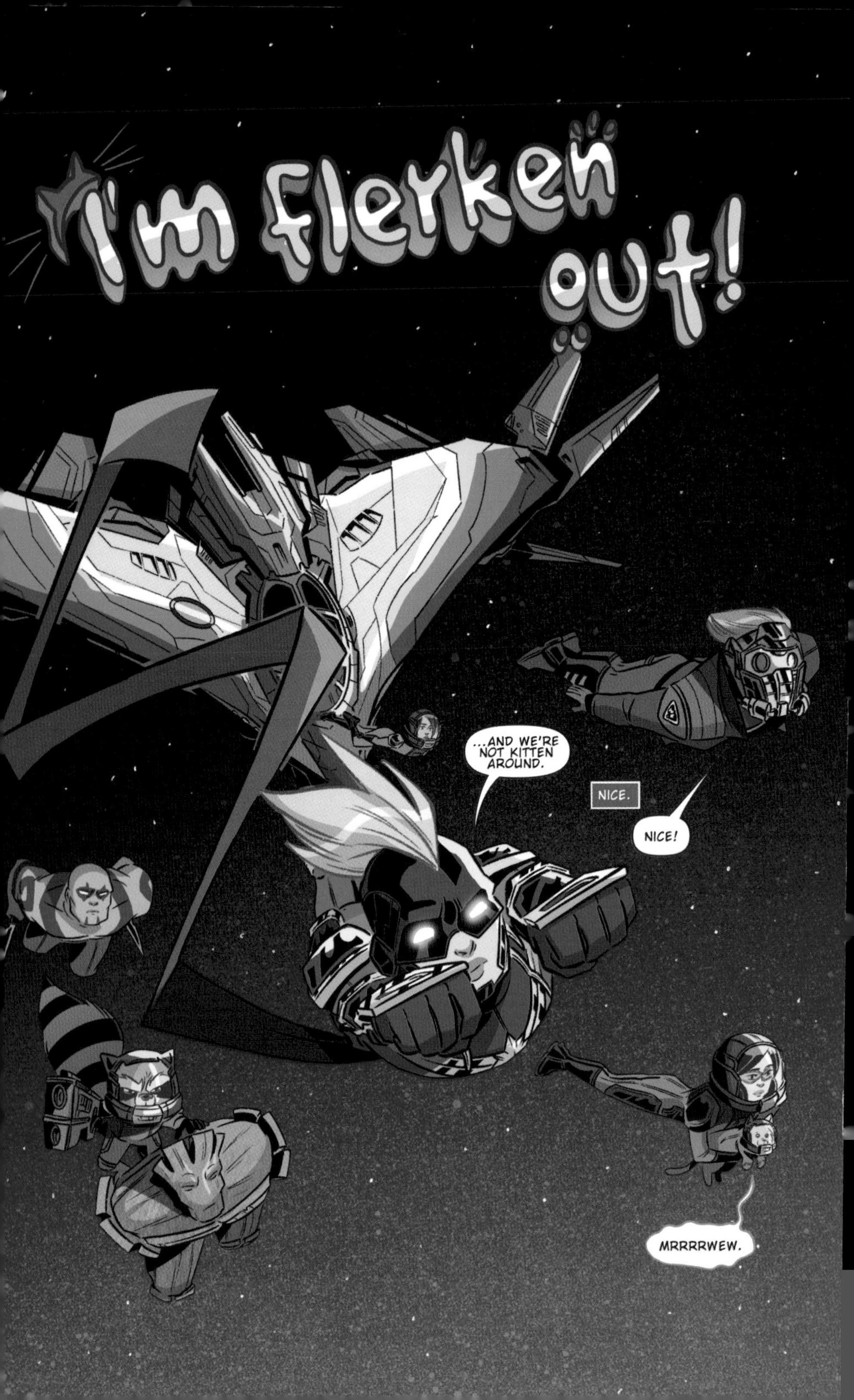
I'm flerken out!
...AND WE'RE NOT KITTEN AROUND.
NICE.
NICE!
MRRRRWEW.

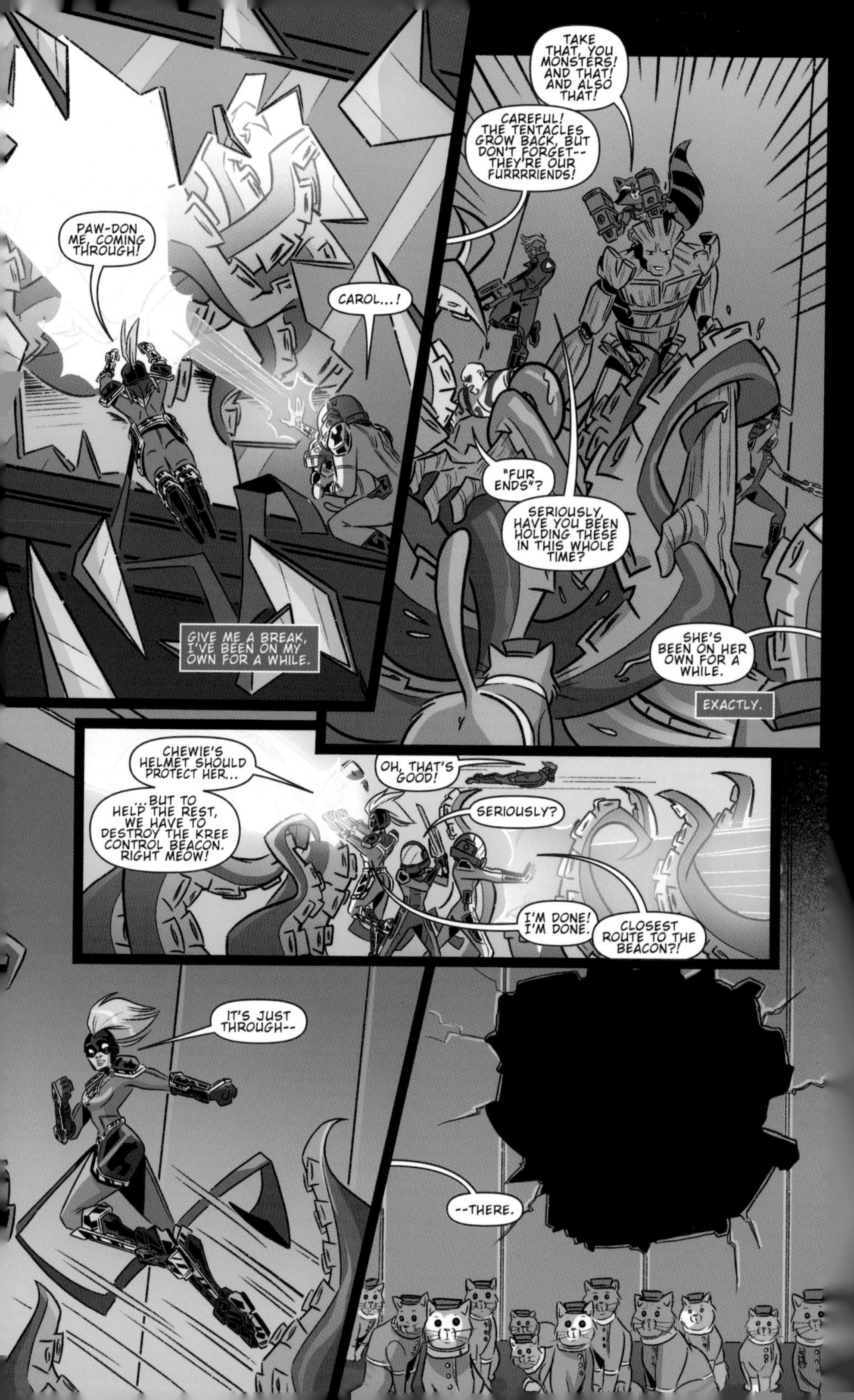
PAW-DON ME, COMING THROUGH!
CAROL...!
GIVE ME A BREAK, I'VE BEEN ON MY OWN FOR A WHILE.
TAKE THAT, YOU MONSTERS! AND THAT! AND ALSO THAT!
CAREFUL! THE TENTACLES GROW BACK, BUT DON'T FORGET-- THEY'RE OUR FURRRRIENDS!
"FUR ENDS"?
SERIOUSLY, HAVE YOU BEEN HOLDING THESE IN THIS WHOLE TIME?
SHE'S BEEN ON HER OWN FOR A WHILE.
EXACTLY.
CHEWIE'S HELMET SHOULD PROTECT HER...
...BUT TO HELP THE REST, WE HAVE TO DESTROY THE KREE CONTROL BEACON. RIGHT MEOW!
OH, THAT'S GOOD!
SERIOUSLY?
I'M DONE! I'M DONE.
CLOSEST ROUTE TO THE BEACON?!
IT'S JUST THROUGH--
--THERE.

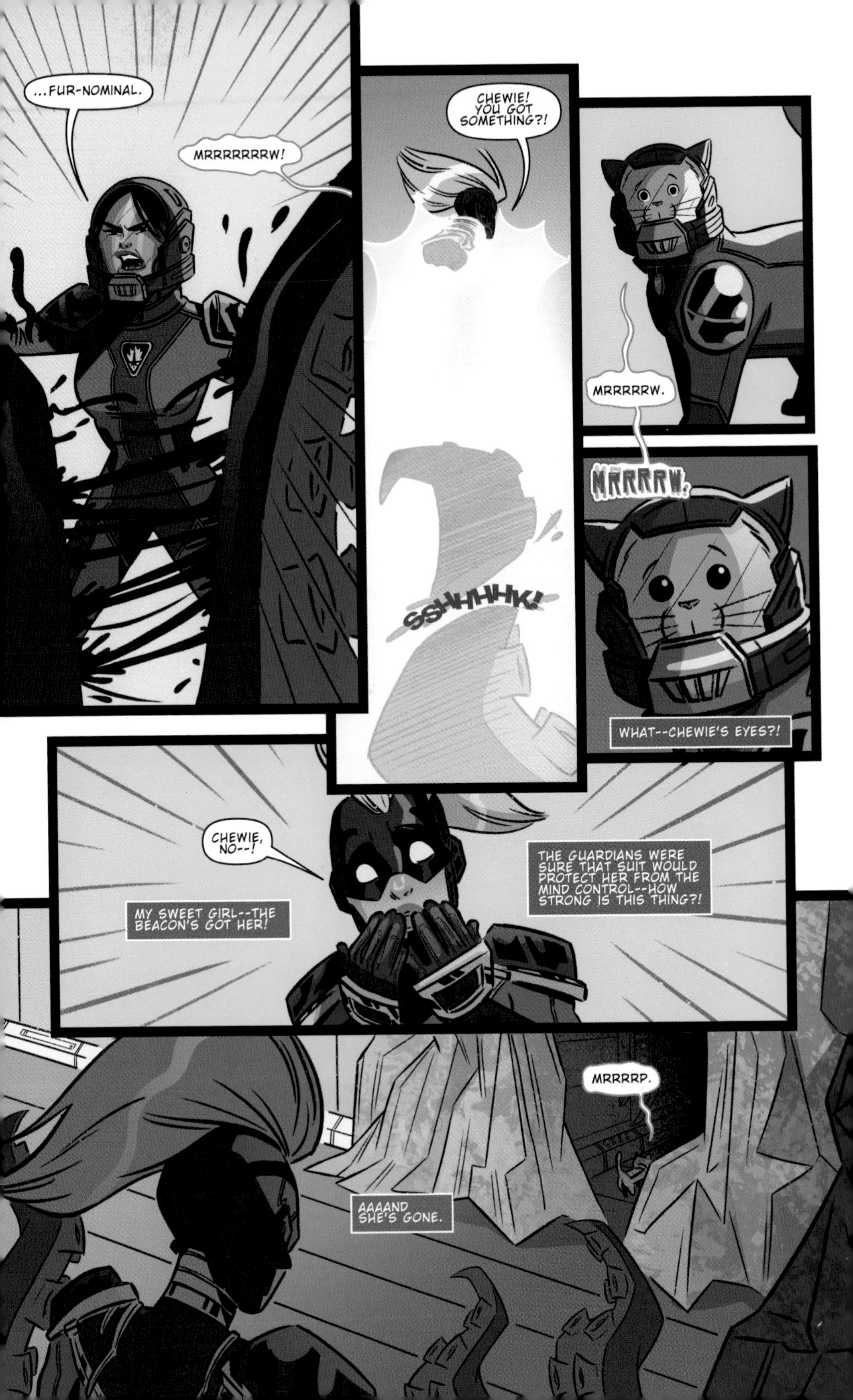
...FUR-NOMINAL.
MRRRRRRRW!
CHEWIE! YOU GOT SOMETHING?!
SSHHHHK!
MRRRRRW.
MRRRRW!
WHAT--CHEWIE'S EYES?!
CHEWIE, NO--!
MY SWEET GIRL--THE BEACON'S GOT HER!
THE GUARDIANS WERE SURE THAT SUIT WOULD PROTECT HER FROM THE MIND CONTROL--HOW STRONG IS THIS THING?!
MRRRRP.
AAAAND SHE'S GONE.

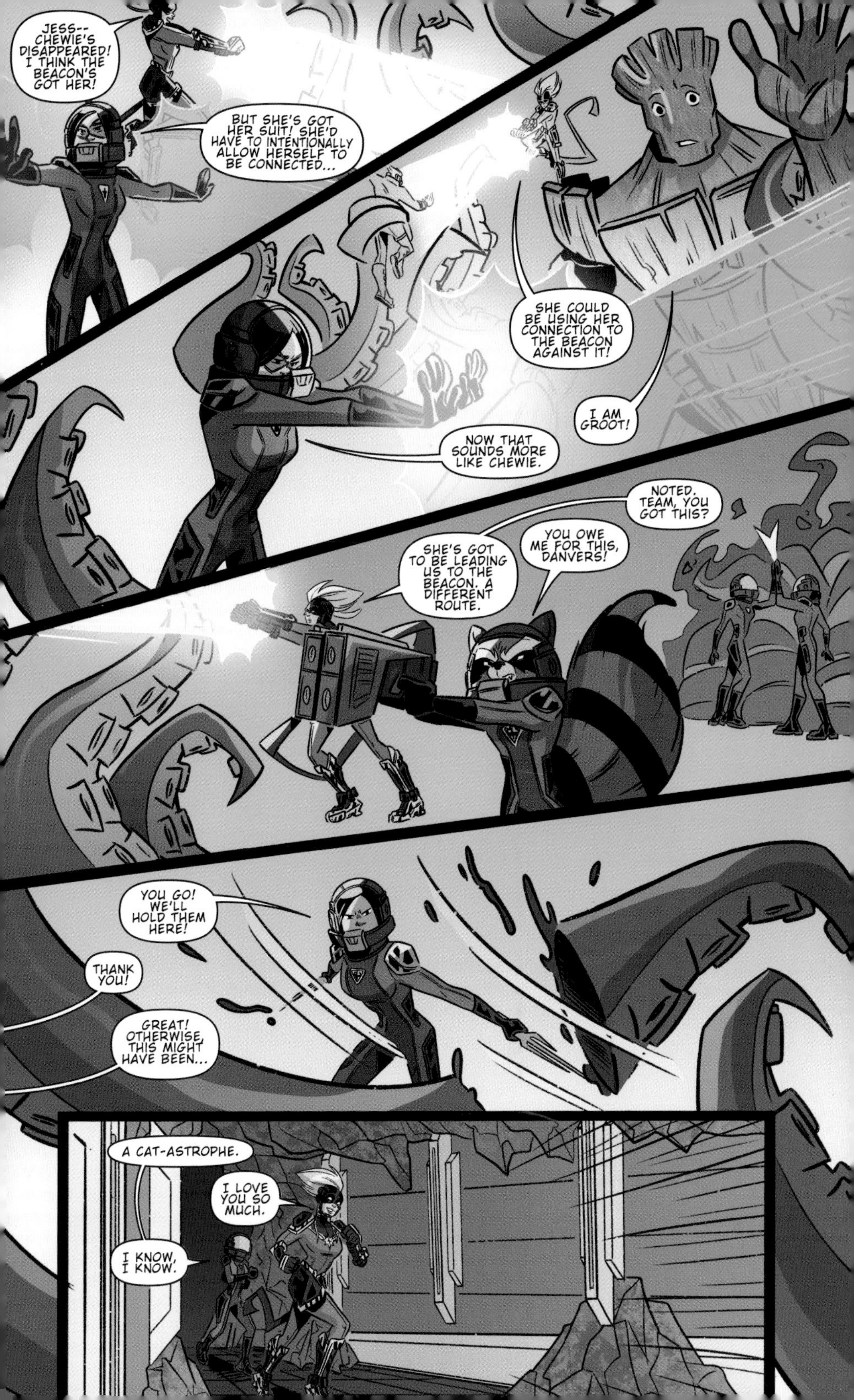
JESS--CHEWIE'S DISAPPEARED! I THINK THE BEACON'S GOT HER!
BUT SHE'S GOT HER SUIT! SHE'D HAVE TO INTENTIONALLY ALLOW HERSELF TO BE CONNECTED...
SHE COULD BE USING HER CONNECTION TO THE BEACON AGAINST IT!
I AM GROOT!
NOW THAT SOUNDS MORE LIKE CHEWIE.
NOTED. TEAM, YOU GOT THIS?
YOU OWE ME FOR THIS, DANVERS!
SHE'S GOT TO BE LEADING US TO THE BEACON. A DIFFERENT ROUTE.
YOU GO! WE'LL HOLD THEM HERE!
THANK YOU!
GREAT! OTHERWISE, THIS MIGHT HAVE BEEN...
A CAT-ASTROPHE.
I LOVE YOU SO MUCH.
I KNOW, I KNOW.

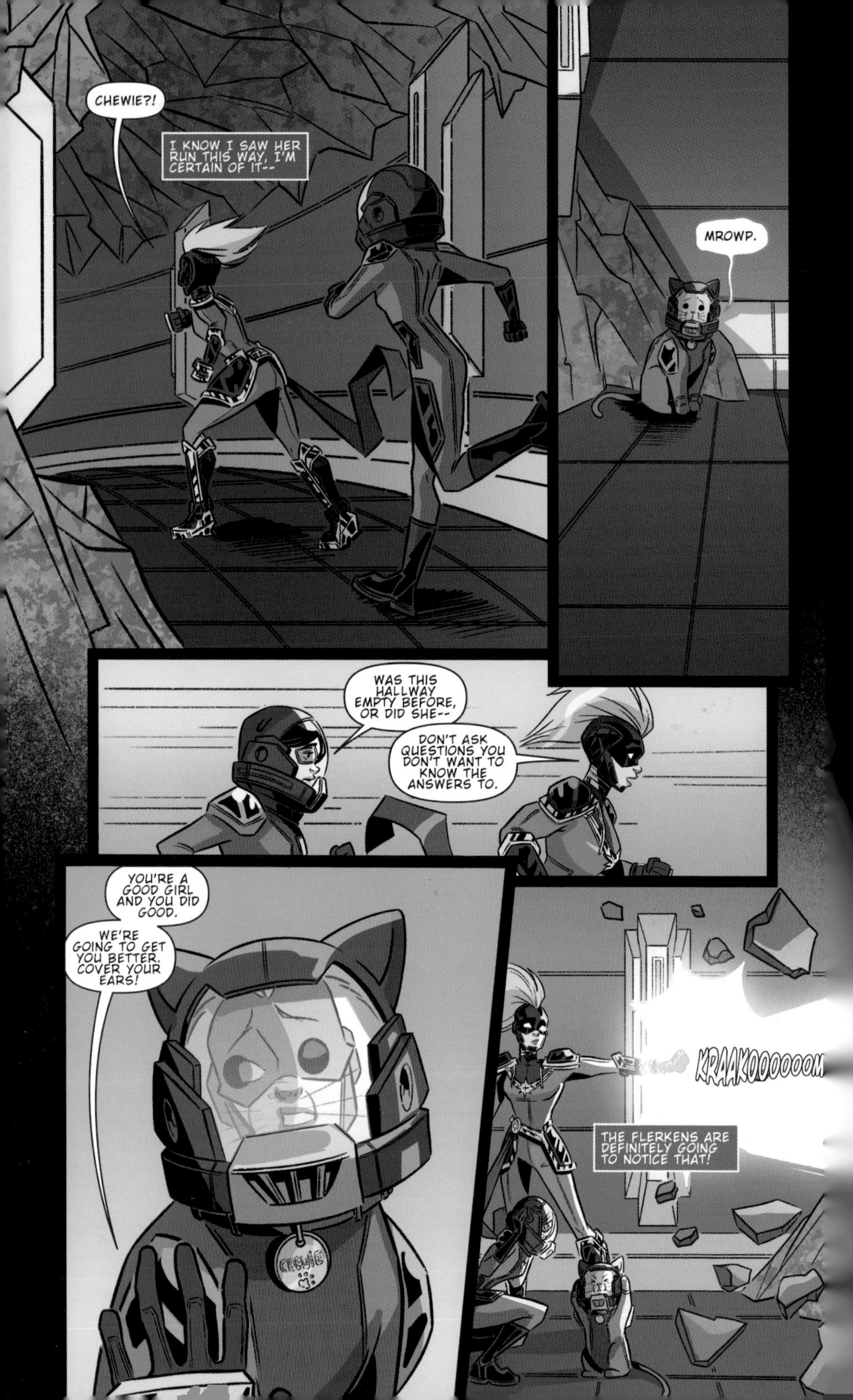
CHEWIE?!
I KNOW I SAW HER RUN THIS WAY, I'M CERTAIN OF IT--
MROWP.
WAS THIS HALLWAY EMPTY BEFORE, OR DID SHE--
DON'T ASK QUESTIONS YOU DON'T WANT TO KNOW THE ANSWERS TO.
YOU'RE A GOOD GIRL AND YOU DID GOOD.
WE'RE GOING TO GET YOU BETTER. COVER YOUR EARS!
CHEWIE
KRAAKOOOOOOM
THE FLERKENS ARE DEFINITELY GOING TO NOTICE THAT!

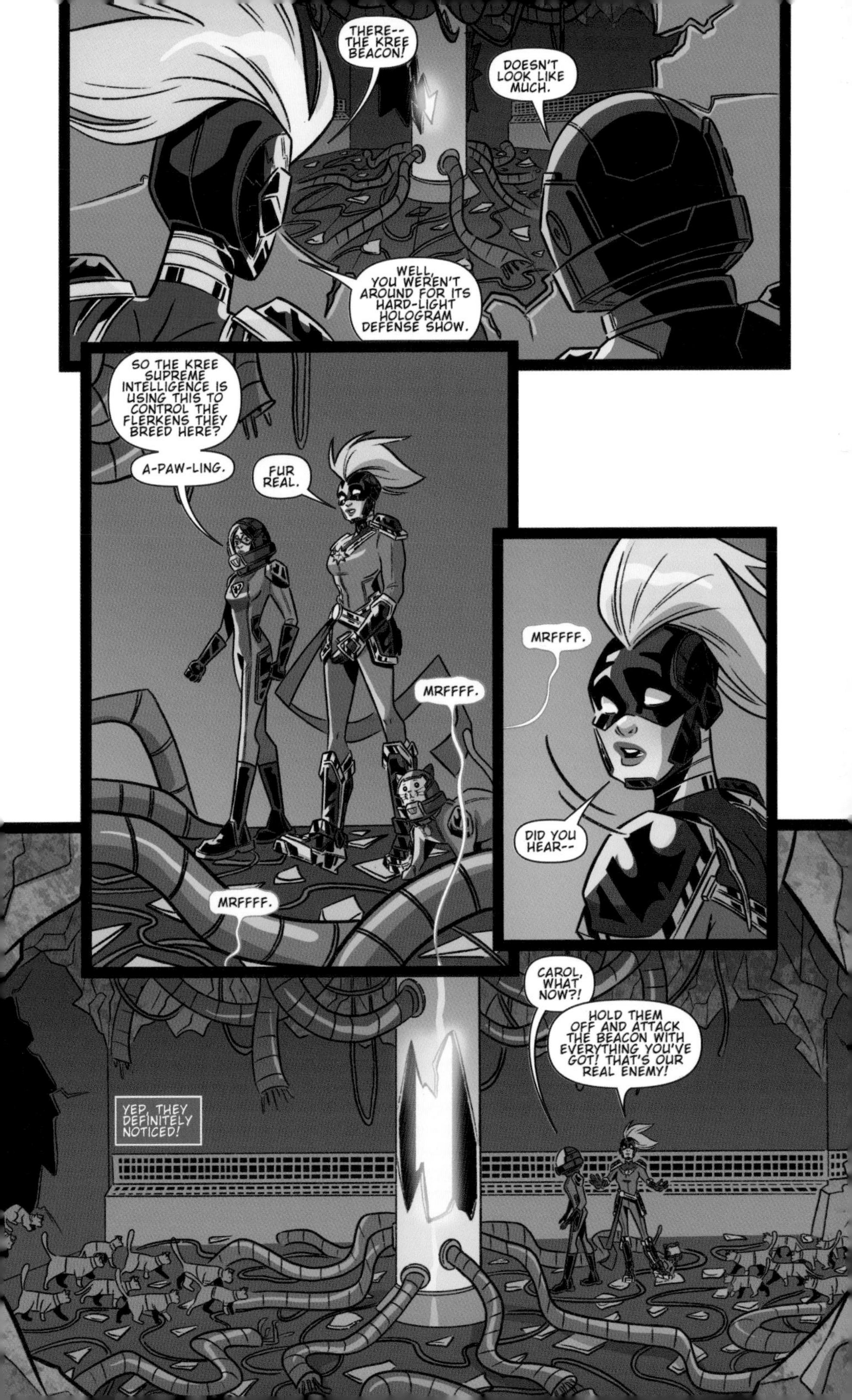

THERE-- THE KREE BEACON!
DOESN'T LOOK LIKE MUCH.
WELL, YOU WEREN'T AROUND FOR ITS HARD-LIGHT HOLOGRAM DEFENSE SHOW.
SO THE KREE SUPREME INTELLIGENCE IS USING THIS TO CONTROL THE FLERKENS THEY BREED HERE?
A-PAW-LING.
FUR REAL.
MRFFFF.
MRFFFF.
MRFFFF.
DID YOU HEAR--
CAROL, WHAT NOW?!
HOLD THEM OFF AND ATTACK THE BEACON WITH EVERYTHING YOU'VE GOT! THAT'S OUR REAL ENEMY!
YEP, THEY DEFINITELY NOTICED!

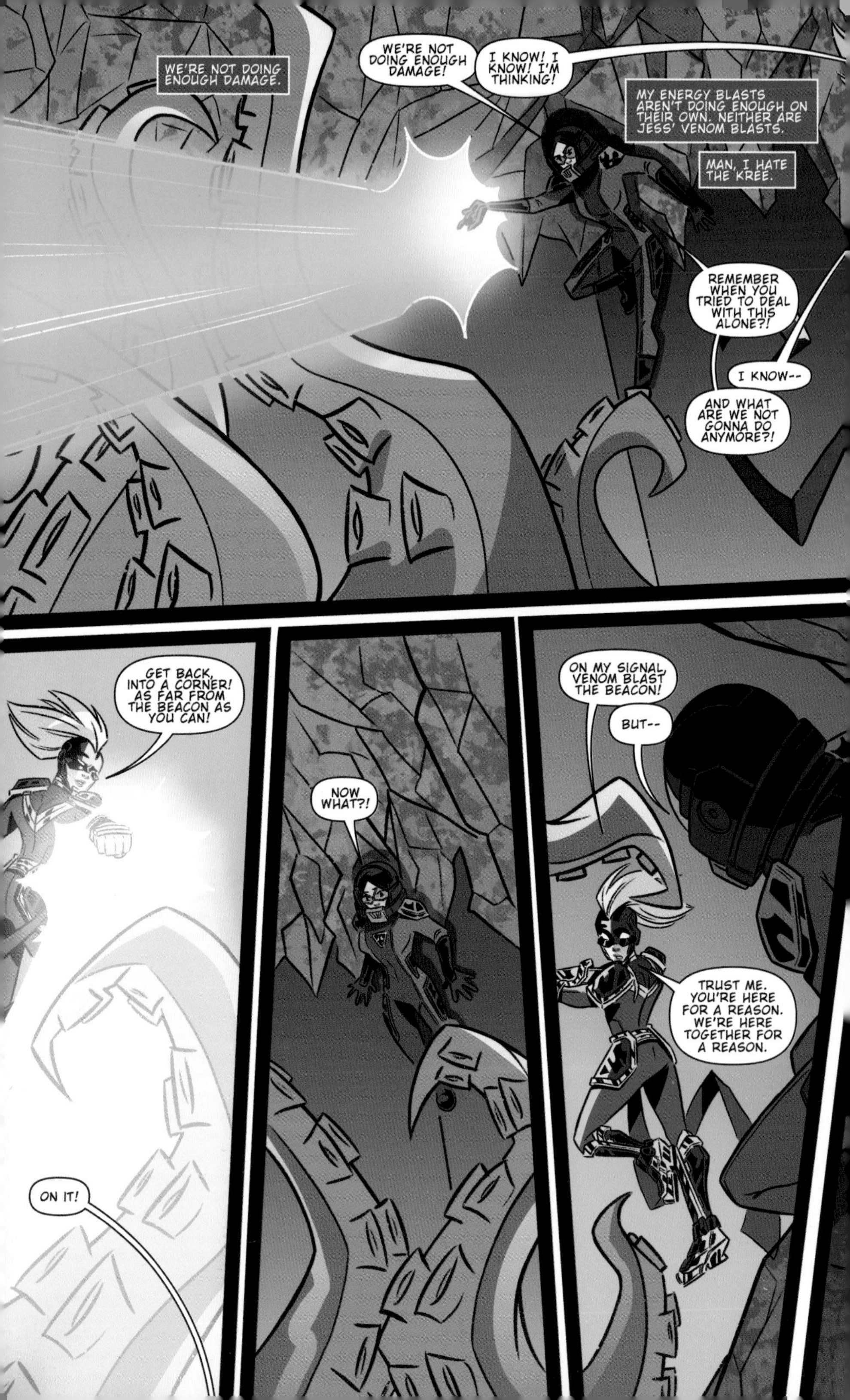
WE'RE NOT DOING ENOUGH DAMAGE.
WE'RE NOT DOING ENOUGH DAMAGE!
I KNOW! I KNOW! I'M THINKING!
MY ENERGY BLASTS AREN'T DOING ENOUGH ON THEIR OWN. NEITHER ARE JESS' VENOM BLASTS.
MAN, I HATE THE KREE.
REMEMBER WHEN YOU TRIED TO DEAL WITH THIS ALONE?!
I KNOW--
AND WHAT ARE WE NOT GONNA DO ANYMORE?!
GET BACK, INTO A CORNER! AS FAR FROM THE BEACON AS YOU CAN!
ON IT!
NOW WHAT?!
ON MY SIGNAL, VENOM BLAST THE BEACON!
BUT--
TRUST ME. YOU'RE HERE FOR A REASON. WE'RE HERE TOGETHER FOR A REASON.

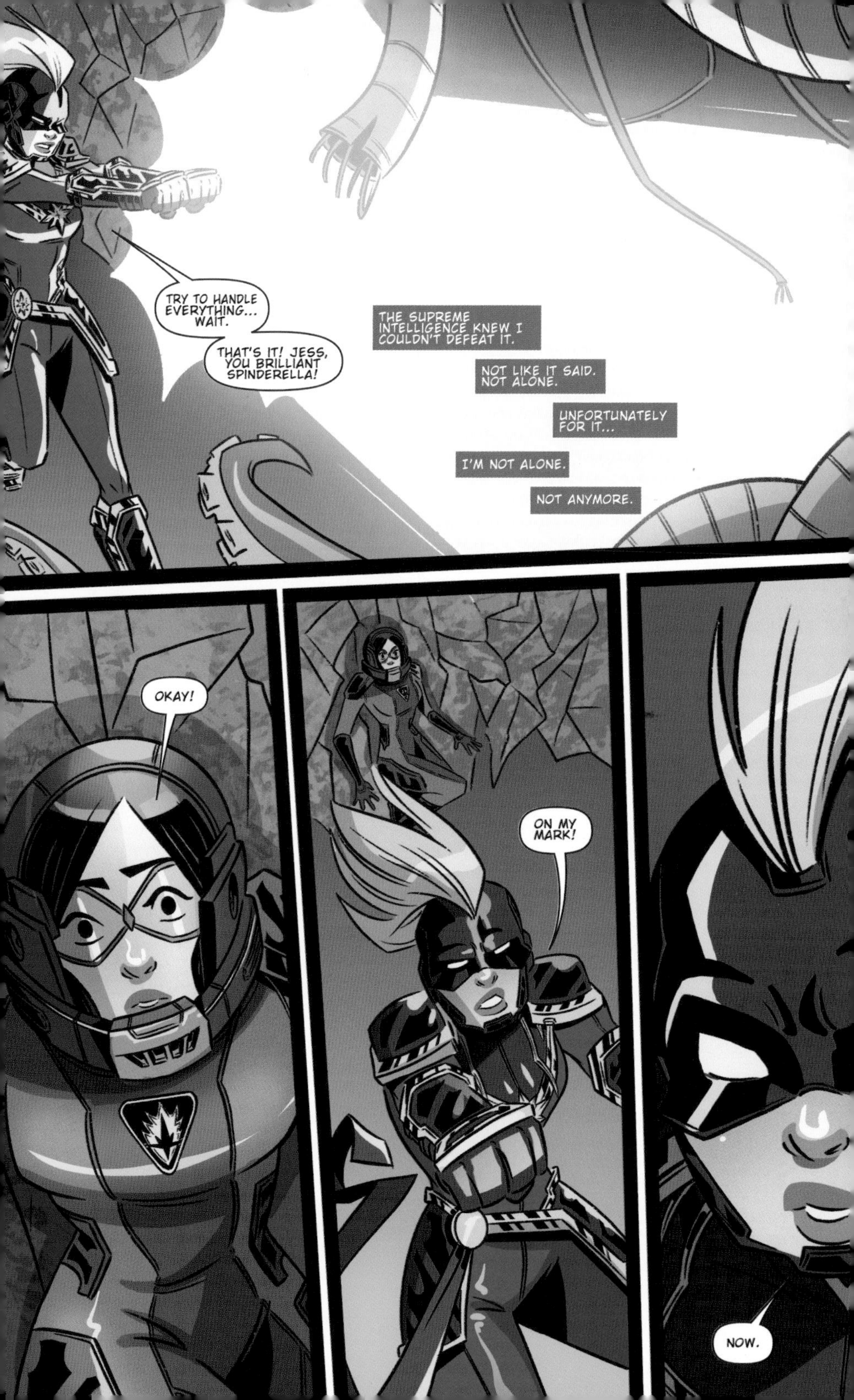
TRY TO HANDLE EVERYTHING... WAIT.
THAT'S IT! JESS, YOU BRILLIANT SPINDERELLA!
THE SUPREME INTELLIGENCE KNEW I COULDN'T DEFEAT IT.
NOT LIKE IT SAID. NOT ALONE.
UNFORTUNATELY FOR IT...
I'M NOT ALONE.
NOT ANYMORE.
OKAY!
ON MY MARK!
NOW.

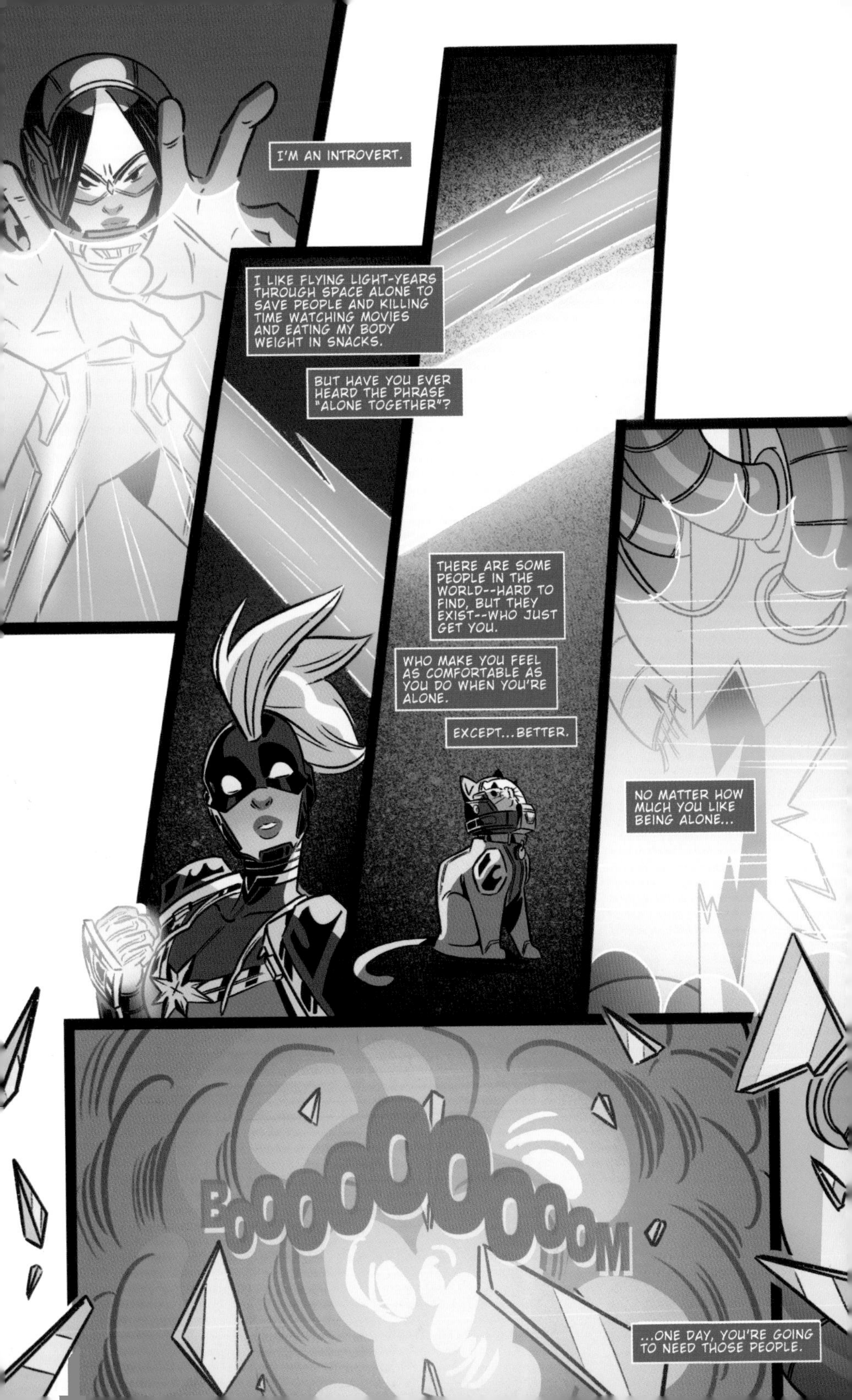
I'M AN INTROVERT.
I LIKE FLYING LIGHT-YEARS THROUGH SPACE ALONE TO SAVE PEOPLE AND KILLING TIME WATCHING MOVIES AND EATING MY BODY WEIGHT IN SNACKS.
BUT HAVE YOU EVER HEARD THE PHRASE "ALONE TOGETHER"?
THERE ARE SOME PEOPLE IN THE WORLD--HARD TO FIND, BUT THEY EXIST--WHO JUST GET YOU.
WHO MAKE YOU FEEL AS COMFORTABLE AS YOU DO WHEN YOU'RE ALONE.
EXCEPT...BETTER.
NO MATTER HOW MUCH YOU LIKE BEING ALONE...
BOOOOOOOOOOOM
...ONE DAY, YOU'RE GOING TO NEED THOSE PEOPLE.

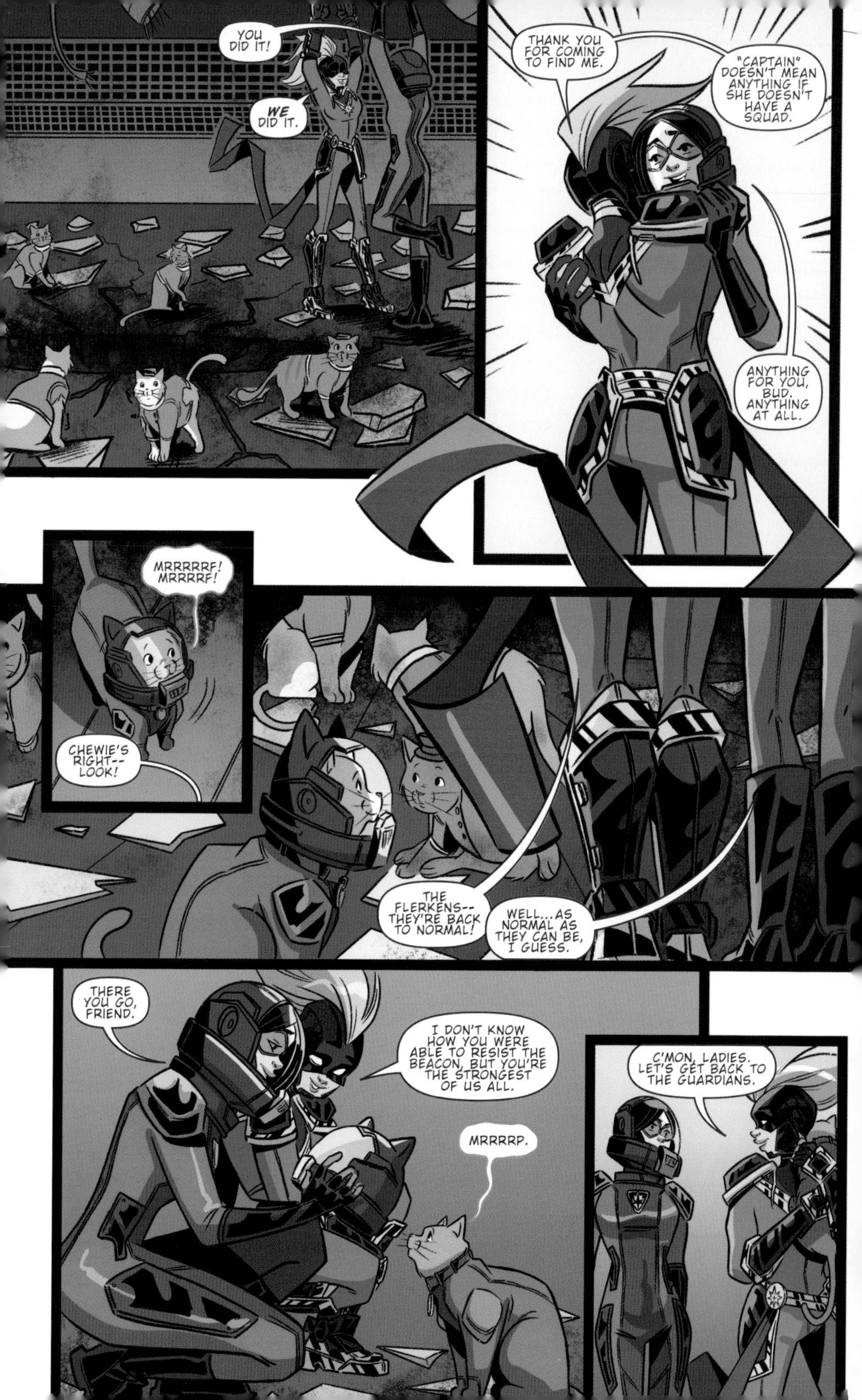
YOU DID IT!
WE DID IT.
THANK YOU FOR COMING TO FIND ME.
"CAPTAIN" DOESN'T MEAN ANYTHING IF SHE DOESN'T HAVE A SQUAD.
ANYTHING FOR YOU, BUD. ANYTHING AT ALL.
MRRRRRF! MRRRRF!
CHEWIE'S RIGHT-- LOOK!
THE FLERKENS-- THEY'RE BACK TO NORMAL!
WELL...AS NORMAL AS THEY CAN BE, I GUESS.
THERE YOU GO, FRIEND.
I DON'T KNOW HOW YOU WERE ABLE TO RESIST THE BEACON, BUT YOU'RE THE STRONGEST OF US ALL.
MRRRRP.
C'MON, LADIES. LET'S GET BACK TO THE GUARDIANS.

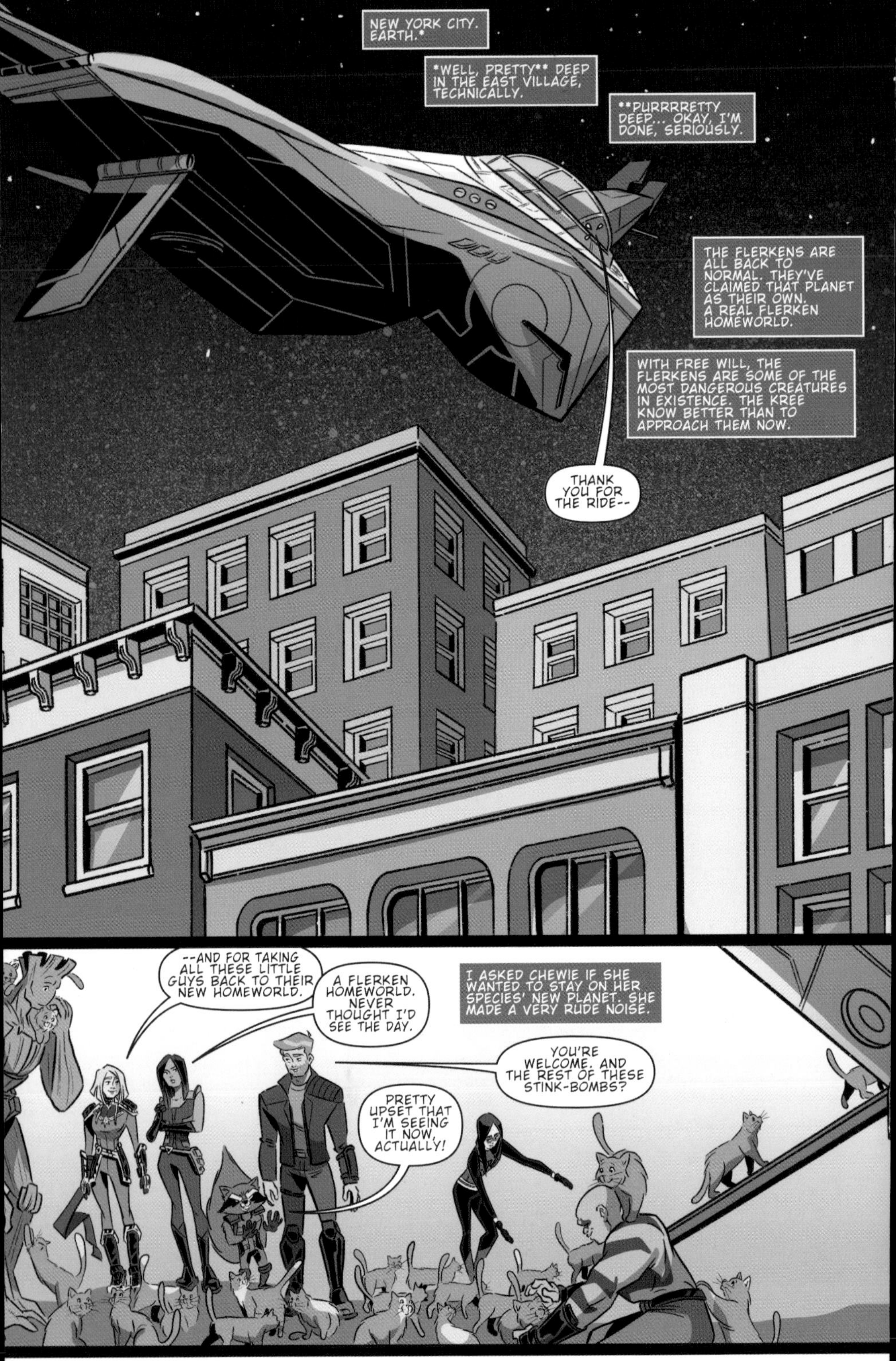
NEW YORK CITY. EARTH.*
*WELL, PRETTY** DEEP IN THE EAST VILLAGE, TECHNICALLY.
**PURRRRETTY DEEP... OKAY, I'M DONE, SERIOUSLY.
THE FLERKENS ARE ALL BACK TO NORMAL. THEY'VE CLAIMED THAT PLANET AS THEIR OWN. A REAL FLERKEN HOMEWORLD.
WITH FREE WILL, THE FLERKENS ARE SOME OF THE MOST DANGEROUS CREATURES IN EXISTENCE. THE KREE KNOW BETTER THAN TO APPROACH THEM NOW.
THANK YOU FOR THE RIDE--
--AND FOR TAKING ALL THESE LITTLE GUYS BACK TO THEIR NEW HOMEWORLD.
A FLERKEN HOMEWORLD. NEVER THOUGHT I'D SEE THE DAY.
I ASKED CHEWIE IF SHE WANTED TO STAY ON HER SPECIES' NEW PLANET. SHE MADE A VERY RUDE NOISE.
YOU'RE WELCOME. AND THE REST OF THESE STINK-BOMBS?
PRETTY UPSET THAT I'M SEEING IT NOW, ACTUALLY!

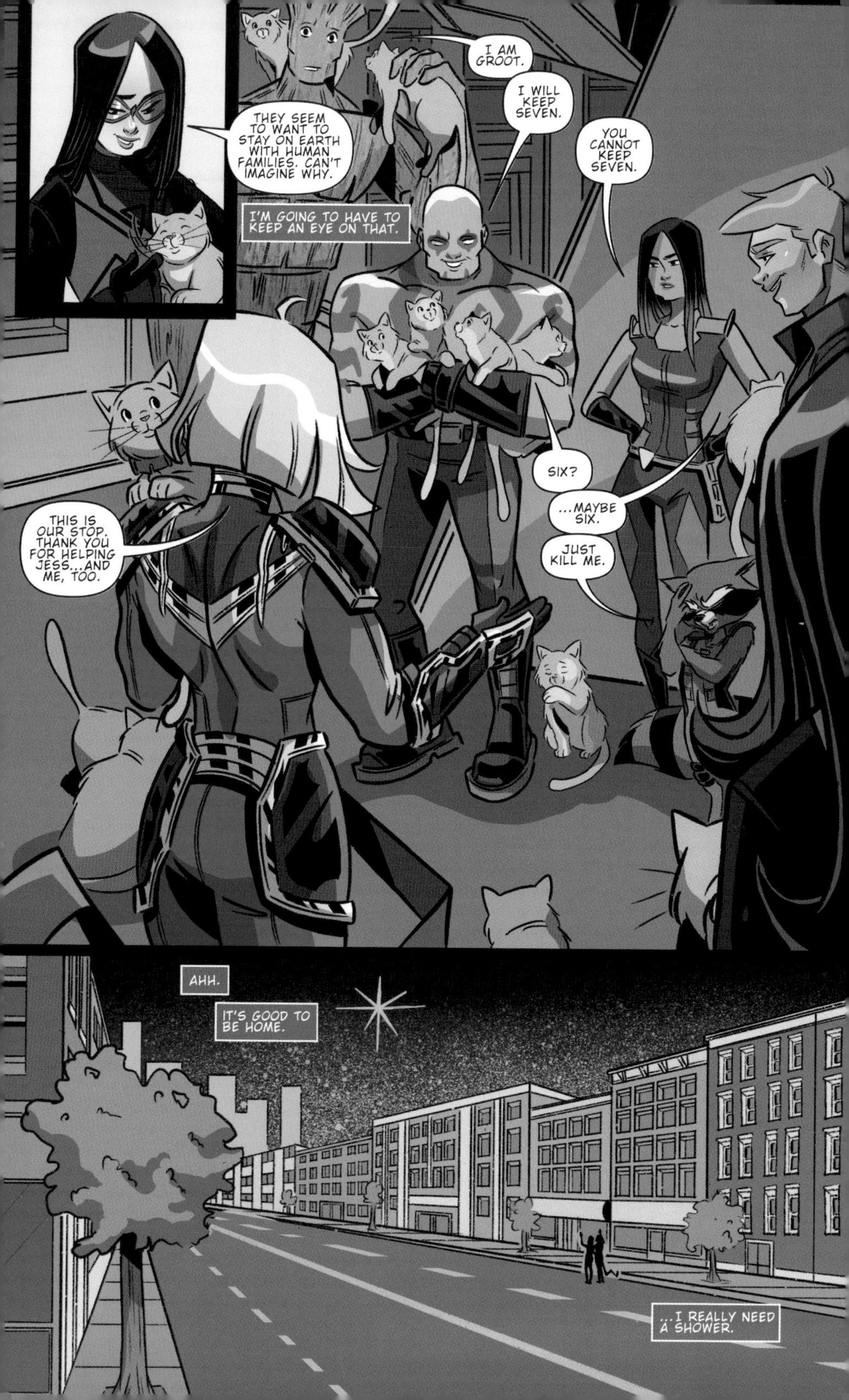
THEY SEEM TO WANT TO STAY ON EARTH WITH HUMAN FAMILIES. CAN'T IMAGINE WHY.
I'M GOING TO HAVE TO KEEP AN EYE ON THAT.
I AM GROOT.
I WILL KEEP SEVEN.
YOU CANNOT KEEP SEVEN.
SIX?
...MAYBE SIX.
JUST KILL ME.
THIS IS OUR STOP. THANK YOU FOR HELPING JESS...AND ME, TOO.
AHH.
IT'S GOOD TO BE HOME.
...I REALLY NEED A SHOWER.

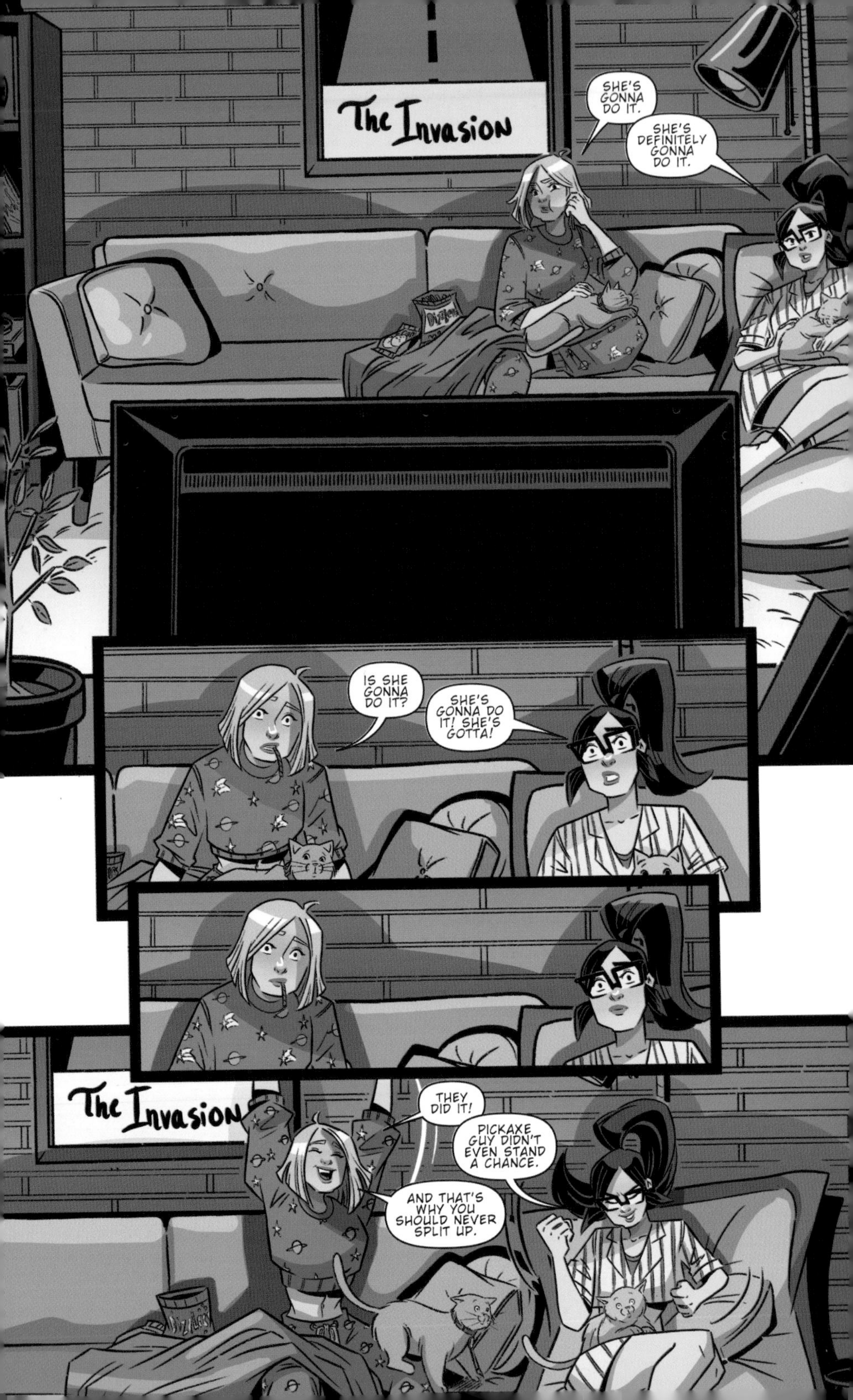
The Invasion
SHE'S GONNA DO IT.
SHE'S DEFINITELY GONNA DO IT.
IS SHE GONNA DO IT?
SHE'S GONNA DO IT! SHE'S GOTTA!
The Invasion
THEY DID IT!
PICKAXE GUY DIDN'T EVEN STAND A CHANCE.
AND THAT'S WHY YOU SHOULD NEVER SPLIT UP.

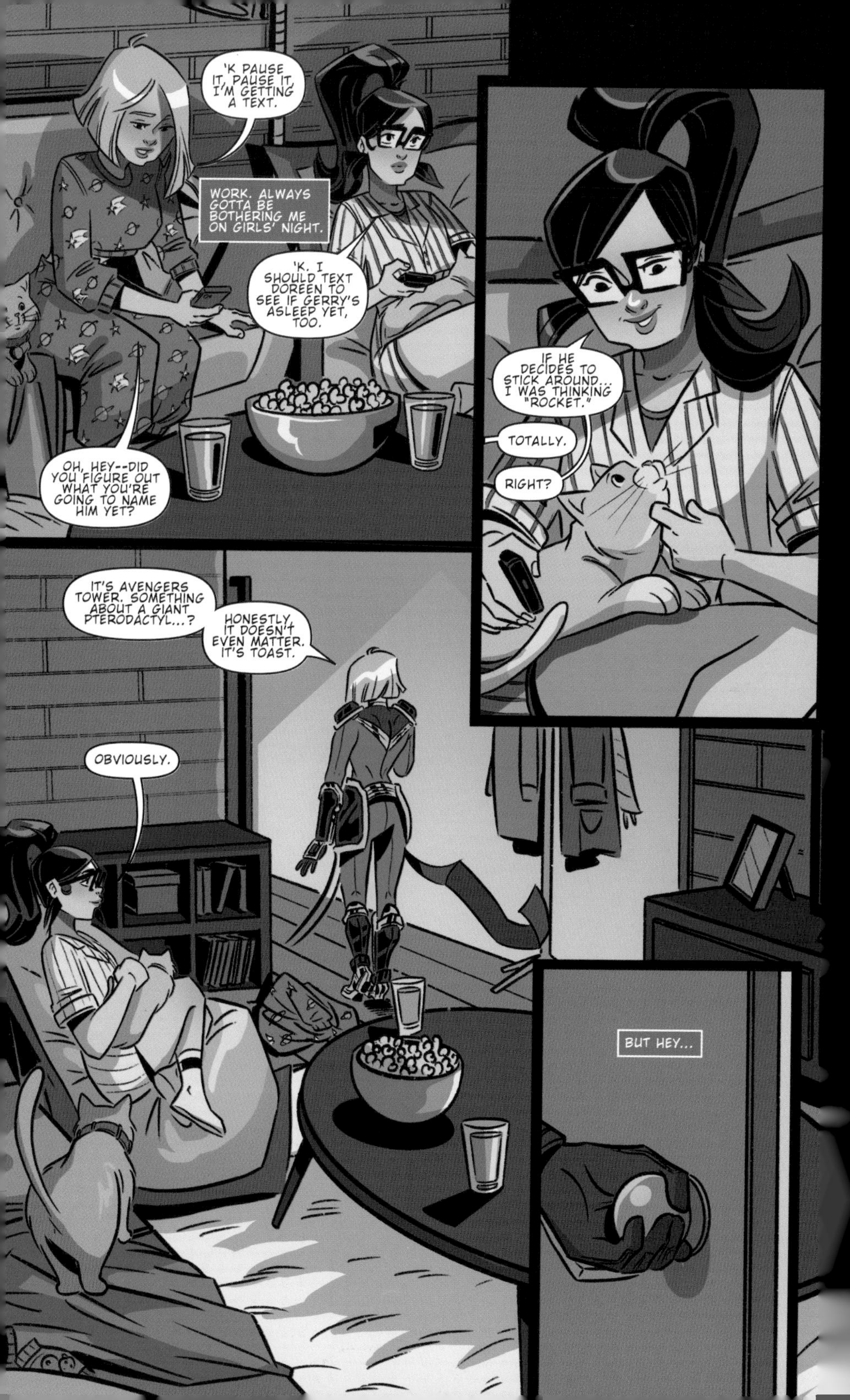
'K PAUSE IT, PAUSE IT, I'M GETTING A TEXT.
WORK. ALWAYS GOTTA BE BOTHERING ME ON GIRLS' NIGHT.
'K. I SHOULD TEXT DOREEN TO SEE IF GERRY'S ASLEEP YET, TOO.
OH, HEY--DID YOU FIGURE OUT WHAT YOU'RE GOING TO NAME HIM YET?
IF HE DECIDES TO STICK AROUND... I WAS THINKING "ROCKET."
TOTALLY.
RIGHT?
IT'S AVENGERS TOWER. SOMETHING ABOUT A GIANT PTERODACTYL...?
HONESTLY, IT DOESN'T EVEN MATTER. IT'S TOAST.
OBVIOUSLY.
BUT HEY...

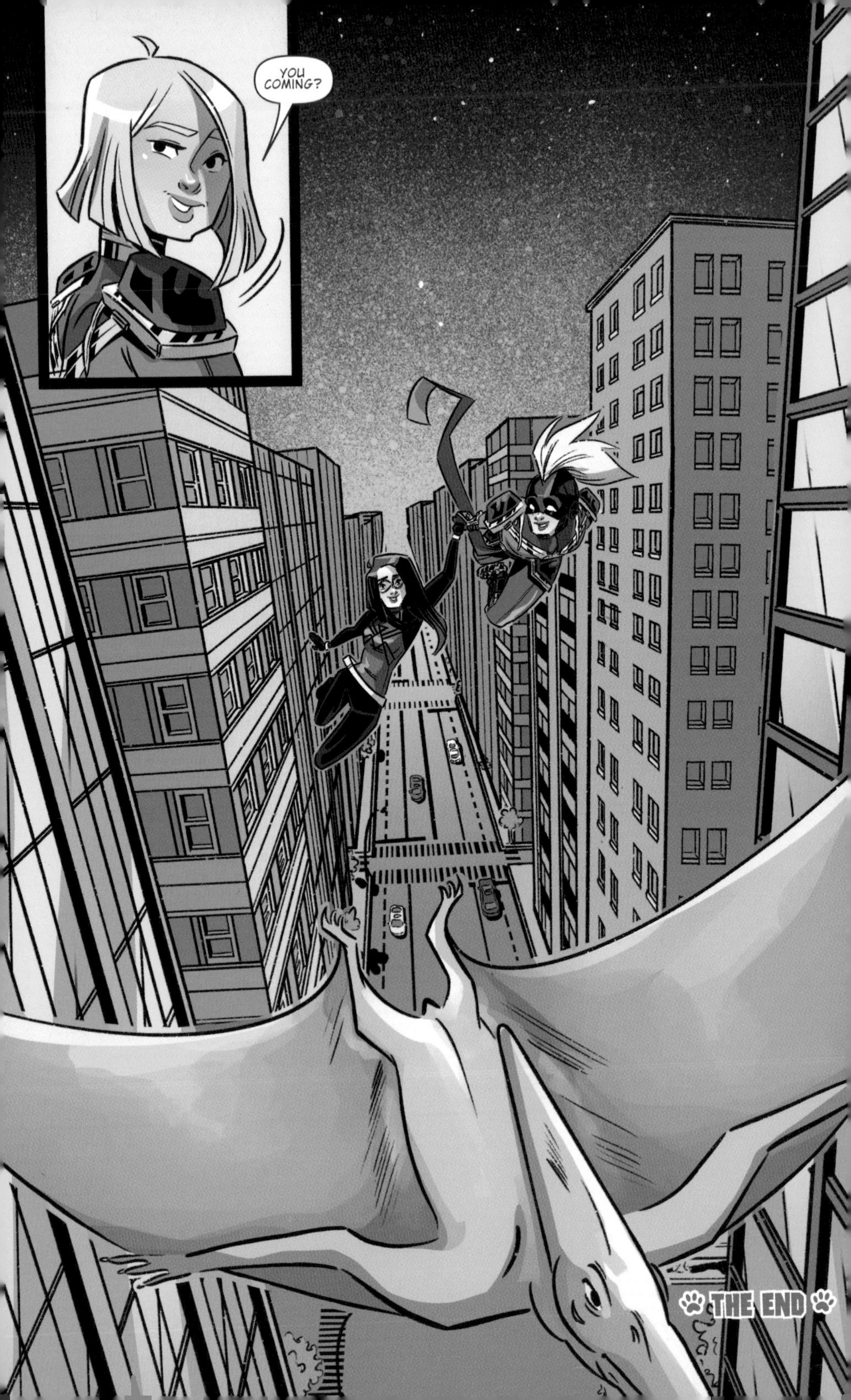
YOU COMING?
THE END

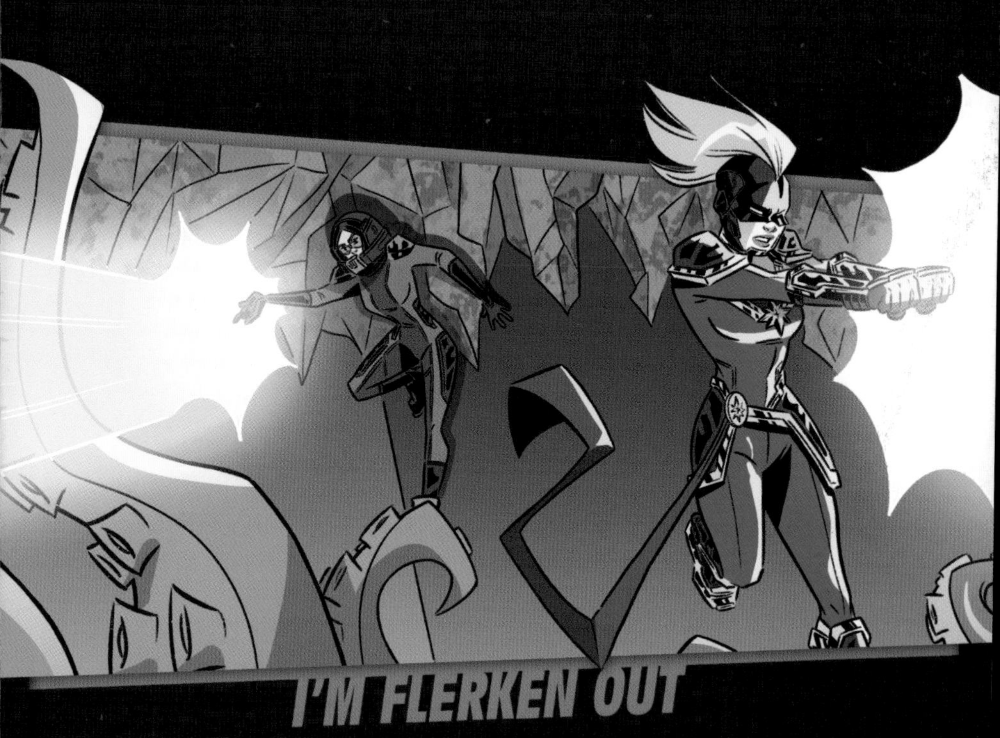
I'M FLERKEN OUT

ART BY: **BRIANNA GARCIA**

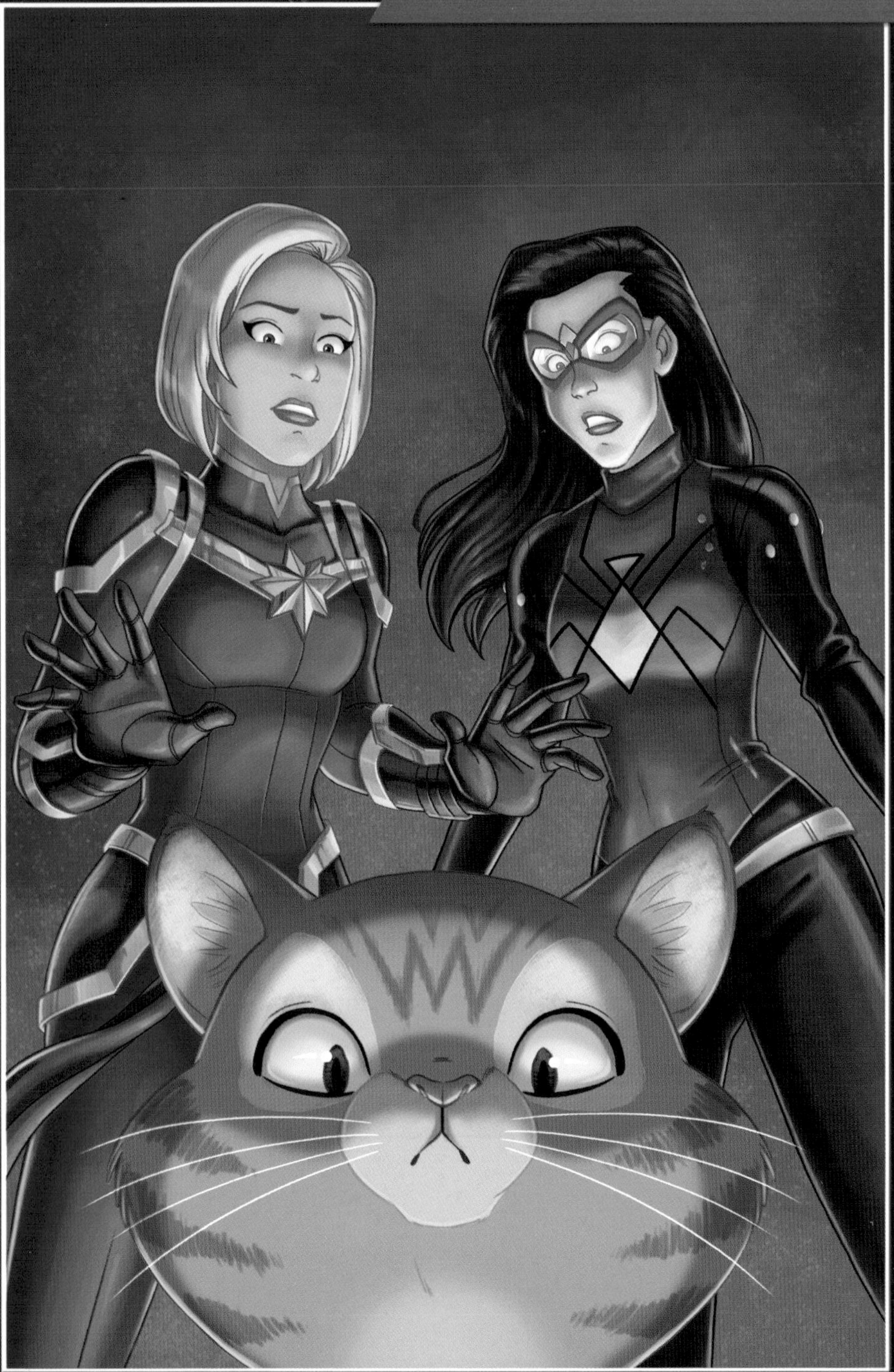

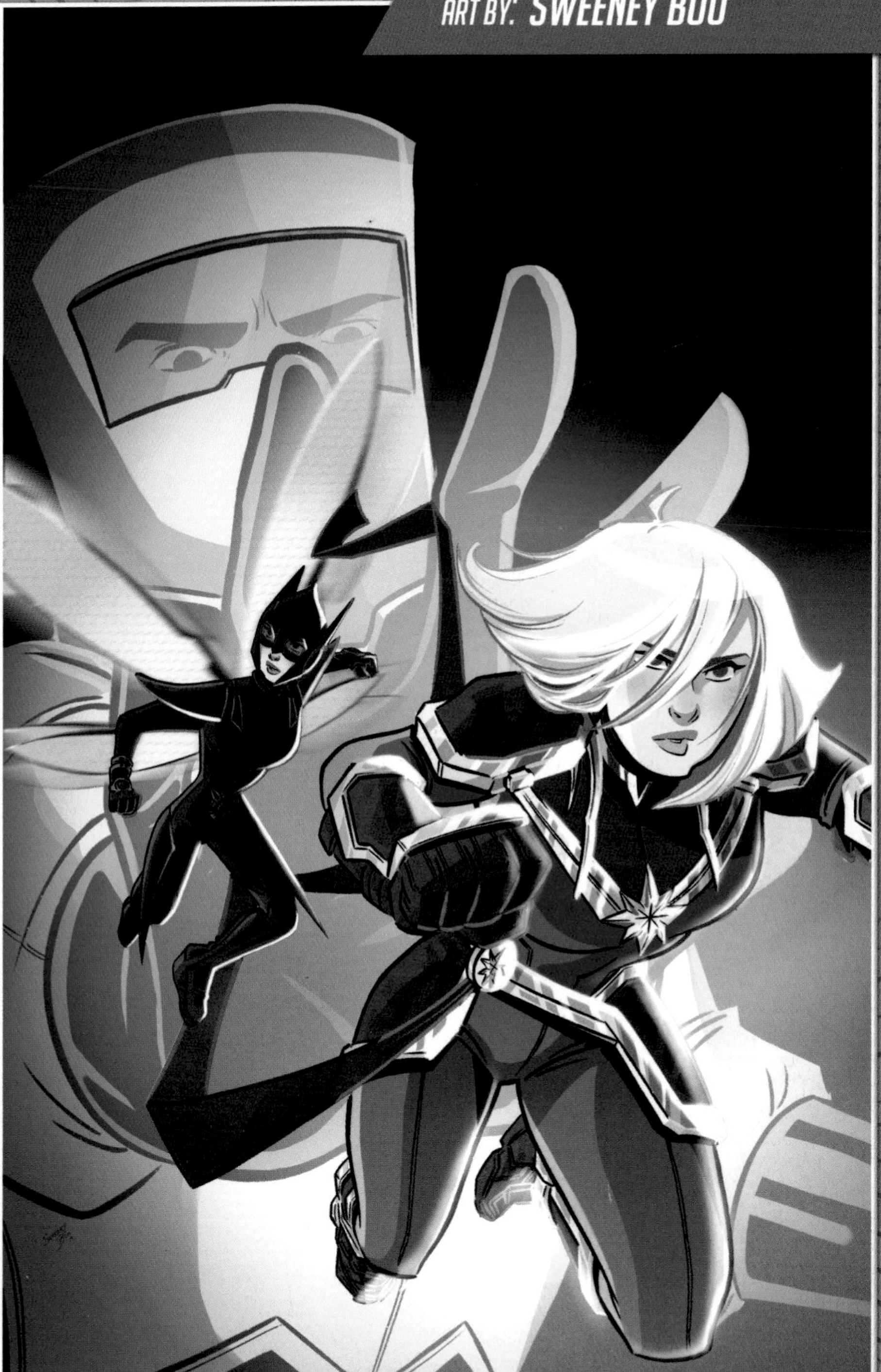

ART BY: SWEENEY BOO

ART BY: KAREN HALLION

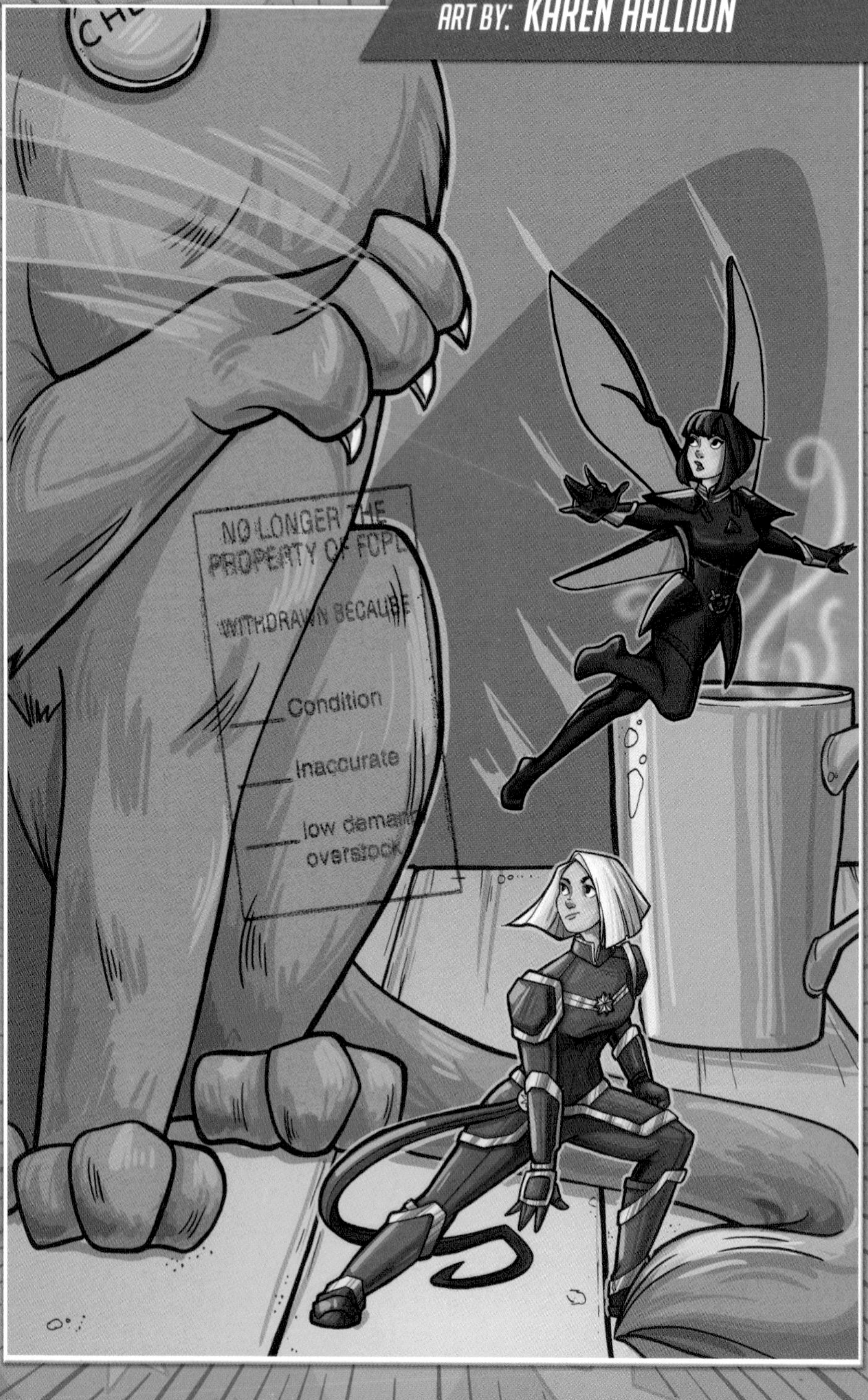